Emotions ruled his thinking.

Now he'd gone from red-hot anger to sizzling need in record time. Wesley took Mary's hand, pulled her down to his eye level and, letting the barrage of desire take over, he kissed her. He forgot about where he sat or why they'd been spending so much time together over the last few days. All he saw was a woman he'd never gotten out of his mind who'd just admitted she still had feelings for him. And he went for it.

As they kissed every obstacle in his head stepped aside. He did what he wanted, took what he wanted, and she met his rough kisses with sweet music in her throat. Her reaction turned him on even more. She'd ignited a fire inside him, and the heat of it, after all this time dormant, shocked him.

"Prove it," he said over her mouth, mid-kiss.

A moment later he stared into her fully dilated pupils, which clued him in that she'd been as much into that kiss as he had.

"Prove that I can still have sex."

Dear Reader,

One of the perks of having a romantic's world view and getting to write books is taking a tough story but featuring the silver lining. When I put my hero Wes in a wheelchair I knew that was the focus I needed to take.

Wes—or the Prince of Westwood, as I like to call him—had it all…and then he didn't any more… and this book focuses on his journey after that. In walks Mary from the other side of the tracks, with her never-say-die attitude, her tiny house on wheels, plus a crazy bargain. And his current world, based on discipline and survivor's grit, gets turned on its head.

Doing research for this book was enthralling, and I was amazed by the leaps that have been made in dealing with spinal cord injuries. Of course this book focuses on Wes and Mary's love story, but I drew so much inspiration from my research and from the people who refuse to limit themselves because of where they sit.

I hope you enjoy the fireworks and the admiration these two meant-to-be lovebirds have for each other as they struggle through to their well-deserved HEA. As I mention in my dedication, I wouldn't have had the guts to bring this story to life without the encouragement of a truly gifted editor: Flo Nicoll.

I hope you enjoy the book!

Lynne

PS Visit lynnemarshall.com for the latest news and to sign up for my newsletter.

MIRACLE FOR THE NEUROSURGEON

BY
LYNNE MARSHALL

First published in Great Britain 2017
By Mills & Boon, an imprint of HarperCollins*Publishers*
1 London Bridge Street, London, SE1 9GF

Large Print edition 2017

ISBN: 978-0-263-06734-7

MIX
Paper from
responsible sources
FSC C007454

This book is produced from independently certified FSC paper to ensure responsible forest management. For more information visit www.harpercollins.co.uk/green.

Printed and bound in Great Britain
by CPI Group (UK) Ltd, Croydon, CR0 4YY

Lynne Marshall used to worry that she had a serious problem with daydreaming—and then she discovered she was supposed to *write* those stories! A registered nurse for twenty-six years, she came to fiction writing later than most. Now she writes romance which usually includes medicine but always comes straight from her heart. She is happily married, a Southern California native, a woman of faith, a dog lover, an avid reader, a curious traveller and a proud grandma.

Books by Lynne Marshall

Mills & Boon Medical Romance

Summer Brides

Wedding Date with the Army Doc

The Hollywood Hills Clinic

His Pregnant Sleeping Beauty

Cowboys, Doctors…Daddies!

Hot-Shot Doc, Secret Dad
Father For Her Newborn Baby

200 Harley Street: American Surgeon in London
A Mother for His Adopted Son

Visit the Author Profile page
at millsandboon.co.uk for more titles.

To Flo Nicoll,
for giving me the courage to write this story,
then helping me make it all it should be.
Having you as an editor has been a blessing.

Praise for
Lynne Marshall

'Emotionally stirring, sensually mesmerising and beautifully written, *His Pregnant Sleeping Beauty* will keep you engrossed until the end.'

—*Goodreads*

CHAPTER ONE

WESLEY VAN ALLEN looked like hell in a shirt. Not even a shirt, a T-shirt. A worn and dingy old white undershirt, with holes, that would be better suited for dusting furniture than wearing. Plus, it was wet, and he was obviously sweaty.

On second glance he looked more like hell on wheels with that driven dark stare. The pride Mary Harris had always admired in him was still in fine form, and so was that glint in his gaze. From the looks of the bulging veins on his deltoids and biceps she must have interrupted his gym time.

Mary bent and lightly kissed his cheek. "Remember me?" Yeah, he'd definitely been working out.

"How could I forget a pest like you?" Looking

surprised, he used the hand towel from his lap to wipe his neck, as he gave her a lazy smile.

When he'd first opened the door, she'd had to adjust her gaze downward to accommodate his being in the wheelchair. His nearly black hair was longer than she'd ever seen it, and she had to admit it looked sexy all damp in disarray. For a man who'd always been proud to a fault and strutted around, letting the world know it, his posture hadn't changed…from the waist up, anyway. But strutting was no longer possible.

Those once sparkling, take-on-the-world eyes Mary remembered as pale brown, coffee and cream, to be exact, seemed darker, more intense than ever. The way they examined her now, made her question why she'd dared to come here today.

She instantly remembered, he'd become a man who'd nearly lost it all. One who worked every day, far too hard, to regain his balance, or so she'd been told.

Mary fought every muscle on her face to hide her sorrow over the guy she'd once known versus the man she saw now, fearing her eyes would betray her. *Do not cry. Do not.*

She forced a bright smile. "I've come to see if I can be of any help. I am an expert, you know."

He could probably see right through her, but she was determined to pull this off.

Alexandra, Wesley's sister, had contacted Mary when the accident had first occurred nine months ago—the shockwave had hit so hard she could barely walk the rest of that day, her chest felt caved in, crushing her heart for the man she'd never gotten to know like she'd once dreamed she might. Mary had just signed on for a six-month hospital physical therapy position in Bangor, Maine, when he'd had his waterskiing accident. Far across the country, she couldn't get home to see him. But she'd mourned his loss, and had worried about him every day, until Alexandra had assured her he was out of danger. Though he would never walk again.

How many times had she wanted to pick up the phone and call Wes, or write him a card expressing her truest thoughts and feelings, but had chickened out because in the end she'd felt she'd had no right? She was just a girl he'd once known. Nothing more.

Alexandra had called again last week, out of desperation, and Mary had heard the panic in her friend's voice. Wes had fired the third home health physical therapy assistant in as many months. "He's taken independence to new heights. No one can stand to be around him!" Alex hadn't known what else to do, so she'd turned to her long-time friend for help.

Though about to sign a contract for another job, this one in New Mexico, Mary had rearranged her work schedule on the spot to get here. That was the beauty of being a free agent, an interim employee, getting to call the shots while traveling the country. But since that phone call, and after not being there for Wes in the beginning, nothing could stop her from helping the man she'd had a crush on since she was fifteen.

"Seriously, what are you doing here?" His unwelcoming tone stung like a paper cut. He rolled his wheelchair backward to allow her to enter. At least that was something.

"I already told you, I'm here to help." She followed him, hiding the hurt from him brushing her off.

"I don't need any help. I've got this." His suspicious gaze seemed to hunt for pity, and if he found it, she knew he'd attack.

She adjusted her over-bright expression to one of questioning. "Really? A guy who's fired three physical therapy aides in three months doesn't need help? I beg to differ." Did she honestly expect him to welcome her when showing up out of the blue?

He *harrumphed* and made a U-turn and continued toward the opposite door in the large and beautifully furnished beach home living room. The ceiling-to-floor windows looked out onto the Pacific Ocean. At the moment it was teal and silver blue, covered with glitter from the sun, and she couldn't avoid noticing. Yet the house felt shut down, dark and lonely, and she wasn't sure if she was supposed to follow him or not. She did anyway, through opened double doors into a huge hallway where a wraparound staircase looked like open arms. Because of his accident, that welcoming entrance would forever be off-limits to him. How awful to be reminded every day in such an in-your-face way.

"I'm serious, Wes, you can't fire the world. It won't bring back your legs." She'd always been one to name the elephant in the room head on, that was if she knew what it was, and in Wes's case she knew exactly why he'd become this guarded and fiercely independent man. He'd become a paraplegic and was dealing with his disability by working too hard, beating the life out of it. And apparently everyone else. No one could keep up with his breakneck schedule, according to Alexandra.

"I don't need you." He spat out the words, reacting to her dose of reality, sounding nothing like the successful neurosurgeon who'd known the course of his life since he'd reached puberty. Who could've predicted this part?

"Alex doesn't agree and she's asked me to help out for a while." When he immediately opened his mouth to protest, she held up her hand to stop him. "Because she loves you."

"Alex needs to mind her own business. She's got her husband and kids to worry about. Tell her I release her of all sisterly responsibility. And you can leave now."

Crushed, Mary laughed, surprising herself. She hadn't seen Wesley in ten years, the day Alexandra had gotten married. The day they'd claimed their second mind-boggling kiss and far more, blamed completely on sharing too much champagne. "Not so easy, Wes. I've taken two months off work to come here. I literally picked up my home and drove from New Mexico to California."

"Why ever would you do that without asking first?"

"Because that's what friends do. Show up to help."

"My friends always ask first." Dismissed.

Another paper cut, this one slicing deeper, drawing more blood. *Do they ever get invited in?*

He might still think of her as a charity case, a stray kitten his sister had once dragged home from public school, but she'd risen above her poverty and all the odds stacked against her. She didn't deserve to be spoken to like that.

"You used to call me kid sister number two. I practically lived with you, Wes. You can't deny you were *all* like a second family to me." She tried to make eye contact, but he didn't co-operate. "Your parents gave me shelter, and you, you insisted I make something of myself." He'd told her that the night he'd *been volunteered* to take her to the prom. She stepped closer to him, hoping with all of her heart she could get through to him. "Well, I have. I've got a freaking PhD, and now I'm here for you, one doctor to another." Funny how life worked out that way.

"So this is payback?" He looked directly at her, taunting her with hurtful insults to give up and leave him alone. "I don't need your help. Thank you, though."

He rolled toward a wall unit lift to take him and his wheelchair upstairs, intent on leaving her standing there, openmouthed. But the snub only gave enough time for fury at being dismissed like a servant to form into words.

"I've been told you're being a total jerk." *Have proof of it firsthand now.* She'd also spoken to his parents before coming. They'd thrown up their hands and moved back to their retirement home in Florida after spending the first six months of recovery with him. “Someone’s got to snap you out of it.”

“Have you been talking to my parents? Dear old Dad, who blames me for what happened? I don’t need toxic people like that around.”

His father may had been the pusher in the clan, but certainly his mother had never been anything but supportive.

“And I’m not like that. Toxic.” Had his father actually blamed him for the accident? Shameful. She’d always known Mr. Van Allen had expected the world of both of his children, but most especially from Wes. He’d raised hell when Alex had changed majors from pre-med to become a dietician, which only required a master’s degree. If Wes had ever dared to venture off his life path, who knows what Mr. Van Allen would have done? Somehow, even back then, she’d sensed that failure was not an option where the Van Allen kids were concerned, but to blame his son for a life-altering accident? Unbelievable.

“Can’t you see I’m doing fine?” He staunchly defended his shutting out the world.

It was time to double down. She knew, though

on the surface Wes looked like he was in fact *doing fine*, he needed assistance from daily PT in ways he didn't even think about, and not just on the parts that were working, but also the muscles and joints in need of passive range of motion. That was something he needed to learn to do for himself, too. And even in the gym, which she presumed from the looks of his upper torso, chest and arms, he did rigorous workouts, someone needed to be standing by in case he got hurt, possibly further injuring his spine. No. She wasn't going anywhere. At least not today. "Have you ever performed surgery without consulting another neurosurgeon first?"

"What's that got to do with this?"

"Everything. You may think you know what you're doing but, whether you know it or not, you need a second opinion."

They shared a ten-second stare down, and he was the first to look away. "Get used to it, Van Allen, I'm not leaving." She waited for him to turn and look at her again. "For the next two months, anyway. In fact, regardless of what you want or think, I'm the best person in the entire world to show up on your doorstep today." Pure bravado. *False bravado.* She caught up to him and placed her hand on his arm to make a point, her knees nearly knocking with insecurity as she did. He jerked at her touch, but didn't yank the arm away.

"There's no doubt you're doing great, but you can't do it all by yourself. You need some supervision with the process. I'm only temporary, but I'm necessary for now. You're a smart man. You know that. So let me help you." To hell with the anxiety summersaulting through her stomach over the possibility of being rejected, his long-term health was more important than her nerves…or her ego. Yet if he told her to leave one more time, she wouldn't be able to justify sticking around.

He shook his head, looking irritated. Something told her to intercept his thought before he said it, to state her case one last time, this time pulling out all the bells and whistles.

"It's because of you that *I'm* the perfect person to help." She tried to keep eye contact, even though matching his resolute stare made her ankles wobbly. "Wasn't it you who told me to make something out of myself? To not let my parents and poverty hold me back? Well, here I am, a bona fide physical therapist, with a doctorate degree, at your service. I understand it may come as a surprise, but I just might know a little about what you need at this point in your recovery. And I don't intend to leave before you're back on your feet." Damn, she'd said the wrong thing! She saw his jaw twitch. Without intending to, she'd delivered her own paper cut. "Metaphorically speaking." It was too late—she couldn't retract the stupid and insensitive phrase.

"For a second I thought you were selling yourself as a miracle worker." He let out an exasperated huff of air, like she'd solicited a service he didn't want or need—subscribe to this magazine or donate to this cause—but felt obligated to take anyway. "If this is your sales pitch, I suppose I have to pay?"

"No!" She was making a total mess of everything, but couldn't back down now. "Let's get that straight from the start. *I don't work for you.* I'm here as a *friend.*" *That way you can't fire me!*

"And where do you expect to live?"

"I've got that all taken care of."

He sat quietly, offering a dead stare in her vicinity, along with a sigh. "Suit yourself," he said, as though he couldn't care less, and continued on toward the wheelchair lift. "I'm going to the gym."

Dismissed again. *Well, not so fast, buddy.* "I'll be back at eight o'clock tomorrow morning to begin your therapy. In the meantime, do you have a groundskeeper? I need some help with something."

He tossed her a quizzical glance, then propelled himself out of the room, calling a woman's name as he did so. "Rita!" His housekeeper? Once she'd come out from the far recesses of the kitchen, making Mary wonder exactly how big the house was, he gave a quick instruction for her to find someone named Heath, as he rolled his chair onto the lift and began ascending the stairs.

Rita tipped her head at him and passed an inquisitive gaze at Mary. "I'll call him now."

"Thanks. I'll be on the porch."

She stepped outside the front door, her hands

shaking, her body quivering. She leaned against the wall biting her lip, blinking her eyes, until sadness overtook her. The man she'd idolized as a teenager was sentenced to a wheelchair for the rest of his life. She'd known it in advance, of course, but seeing him—the same yet so changed—drove the point home and deep into her heart.

The ocean blurred, her skin flushed with heat, and her pulse jittered, forcing her to let go of the threatening tears. To stop fighting and release them before she choked and drowned on them. It had been a long time since she'd cried, and they pricked and stung the insides of her eyelids. She buried her face in the bend of her arm, smothering the sudden keening sounds ripping at her throat, thankful the screeching seagulls overpowered her mourning.

Wesley took a break from his demanding workout routine and peered out the upstairs window, not believing what he was seeing. Heath, his groundskeeper, directed Mary as she backed a tiny portable wood-covered house, complete with porch—if you could call that a porch—onto the graveled ground beside his unattached garage. *So that's how she'd taken care of living arrangements.* She drove the pickup truck like a pro, threw it into park and jumped out to check her handiwork. Clearly satisfied with the parking job, she dusted her hands and went about releasing the house from the towing hitch.

This wasn't her first time at that rodeo.

His guess was that the RV-sized house couldn't be more than two hundred square feet, tops. Sure, Mary was petite, no more than five-three and a hundred and ten pounds wringing wet, but it had to be snug in there. Why would she want to live like that for two months?

She smiled, and from all the way upstairs he could see the self-satisfaction in her expression. Determination had always been her saving grace, and he'd admired it. Until just now when she'd trained her grit on him and weaseled her way back into his life. He didn't need anyone—didn't his family get it? He shook his head, frustrated yet amused. That same tenacity had always been the key to her survival. Could he fault her for not letting him send her away?

He moved further into his gym and grabbed some free weights.

Mary had gotten a lousy start with her parents stumbling their way through life, blaming everyone and everything else on their failings, rather than taking a good look at themselves. Fortunately, she hadn't picked up their lax habits. In fact, she'd done exactly the opposite—she'd taken a long look at her parents and had become convinced she could do better for herself. Then she'd set out to prove it. And prove it she had. She held a doctorate degree. Could work anywhere she wanted. And at this point in time she'd chosen to work here. Lucky him.

When Alexandra had first brought her home, Mary had been scrawny and had worn clothes from thrift shops. They'd been assigned to work on a science project together, and instead of judging Mary on her appearance Alex had been raised to be open-minded. She'd treated Mary like all of her other friends, though those friends had all been rich. Without passing judgment, Alexandra had quickly zeroed in on how bright Mary was—beyond how nice and sweet she was—and their team project had taken first place. She'd also realized that Mary couldn't always depend on meals at home so she'd quickly become a regular guest for meals at the Van Allen house. Soon Mary had become best friends with his big-hearted sister.

Back then, he'd also been taken in by Mary's upbeat spirit, and secretly by her waist-long strawberry blonde hair, which she wore only shoulder length these days. Her shining inquisitive green eyes had stood out like a newly discovered gem in a household of brown-eyed people, and he'd been drawn to her from their very first meeting. Plus, he'd seen something else in that wide and intelligent stare of hers—admiration. Admiration for him. He'd enjoyed knowing his sister's new best friend had a huge crush on him, accepted it with pride, even fed that crush from time to time.

But she'd been innocent and vulnerable and, with parents like hers, hungry for love and attention. With a father like his, who had unwavering expectations for him, well, Wes had been wise enough to play gently with Mary's heart by keeping her at arm's length, knowing his future would take a far different direction from hers. Still, selfish eighteen-year-old that he'd been, he'd strung her along, given her enough attention to keep her hopeful.

Damn, he'd been mean even then. Or careless? Egotistical for sure. Hadn't the *Prince of Westwood* been his family nickname? Especially the one time he'd slipped up and let his—what should he call it—curiosity or desire get the better of him.

Long before *everyone* had had a cell phone—especially kids like Mary—and social media had taken hold of the entire world, she'd appeared on their doorstep, breathless and excited. Alexandra hadn't been home—come to think of it, no one else had been either—but he'd invited her in anyway. When he'd seen her disappointment at not having Alex to share her great news with, he'd offered to listen and to deliver the information personally to his kid sister.

Mary had made the principal's list, which would ensure she'd be able to continue on at the

Magnet school for the next year. She'd only been admitted the prior year on that contingency, and because, like most private schools, the school held a certain number of slots for marginal teens like her. Her joy had been contagious and swept up by her beaming smile—the same one she'd tried to flash at him just minutes earlier in his entryway—he'd let down his usual barriers where Mary had been concerned, crossed the line and kissed her.

What had started out as a congratulatory kiss had soon changed into one packed with typical teenage male need and longing that he'd kept hidden since the first day he'd met her. And she'd been a very active participant in that kiss, a kiss so heady he remembered it clearly to this day. If his mother arriving home from her charity meeting hadn't abruptly broken things up, being young and driven by hormones, not to mention dumb enough to let desire take over back then, who knew what might have happened?

He traded in the first weights and lifted two heavier weights and began vigorously trading repetitions, like a locomotion locked in place.

He'd always been lucky that way, saved from his wandering, kept on the straight and narrow if not by himself then by outside forces, especially by his father, because he was meant to be a doctor. And not just any doctor, a neurosurgeon. He'd planned his entire life around it, and a young, pretty and fresh face like Mary's couldn't get in the way. Yes, his parents were open-minded about many things, but getting mixed up with a girl literally from the wrong side of the tracks would never have been tolerated by dear old Dad. Alexandra having Mary as a friend had proved to be charitable enough for the Van Allen family.

Until her prom two years later. When no one had invited Mary the first week after the school prom kick-off announcement, Alexandra had begged Wesley to invite her. He'd fought it at first, knowing there had to be several guys who'd love to take a girl like Mary, unless they were snooty and let her being poor get in the way of good taste. By the end of week two Alexandra had gotten her mother involved, and what had seemed beneath him as a twenty-year-old university student had been foisted on him. Two-three years older than all the others attending, he'd been volunteered to take Mary to the prom.

If he'd let himself look deep down, he wouldn't have been able to deny he still had vague feelings for her. He'd become a sophisticated pre-med student and a seventeen-year-old woman was not only jail bait but socially undesirable. The Prince of Westwood had taken her to the prom anyway, just so his family could wear the "aren't we good people" badge.

His worldly-wise self hadn't expected to be knocked off his feet when he'd seen Mary that night in the dress his mother had bought. Not as pricey or special as Alexandra's dress, of course, but perfectly suited to her. His conscience had been dealt its first blow when he'd picked her up at the ratty mobile home park she'd lived in, her parents not even bothering to make an appearance. Maybe they'd been embarrassed? Regardless, he'd taken Mary back to his house where Alexandra and her friends had waited to take before-prom pictures, wondering how such a lovely flower had grown in such bleak surroundings.

Then he'd spent the entire evening keeping her

at arm's length, being a boorish cosmopolitan-minded university man, The Prince of Westwood lecturing her on making something of her life. Explaining to her how insignificant something like a high school prom registered in the course of a lifetime. *So why was he still thinking about it now?*

While on his soapbox that night, he'd warned her about guys—like himself—who'd love to take advantage of her.

So wise. So stupid. So moved by her poverty. So protective of her. Out of obligation, he'd asked her to dance and when holding her he'd made the mistake of looking into those eyes, a shade darker than her pastel green dress. Innocent and beautiful and calling out to his soul. To love her.

He'd known he couldn't. He hadn't been nearly enough of a man to risk that. When he'd taken her home, out of gratitude she'd thrown her arms around his neck, and he'd nearly kissed her the way he'd wanted to all evening. But he'd known it would change everything if he did, and he couldn't stray from his calling. Nothing could keep him from medical school, and surely getting involved with a girl like Mary would change his life. For the better? Who knew?

How pompous he'd been, lecturing her on making something of her life. To do it for herself because no one else could.

He stopped the repetitions and stared out the gym window down to where her crazy little house stood.

Wes had seen the disappointment in Mary's gaze after their chaste kiss the night of the prom, yet her sweetness had remained. She'd dutifully thanked him and promised not to let him down, playing her "kid sister" role perfectly. Before he'd left, he'd told her how beautiful she looked and even in the dark of night she'd beamed. So princely. Such power. All the more reason to save her from him. Yet he'd walked away wondering who between them had the most power over the other and sure he'd left a piece of his heart behind. Forever.

The least he could do was let her share her expertise with him now. Who knew, he might learn something, and if that helped his recovery and goal to get back to work again, it would be worth all of these memories bombarding him about his unwanted guest.

He'd had enough of the free weights and trained his sight across the room, out of that blasted window…to her house.

Returning to university that next afternoon, it had been easy to brush the moment—their special night—under the table and move on. Not really, but he'd worked at it at least. Truth was he'd carried those memories around with him for a decade until they'd been replaced with an amazing kiss they'd shared at his sister's wedding several years later.

He rolled under the pull-up bar and grabbed hold, lifting himself out of the wheelchair, pressing his chin to the bar, over and over, until sweat rolled down his temples and his arms trembled.

Still on the fast track to success back then, he'd been about to become engaged to Giselle, a young woman of his social standing, with all the proper credentials and diplomas to be a rich doctor's wife and a doctor herself. Plus she'd been vetted by dear old Dad. Yes, the decision had been cold and calculated, but it fit in with his future. To this day, long after his engagement had fallen apart, his medical practice had taken off and his bank account had doubled—but what did success matter anymore?—he'd recalled that champagne-inspired kiss he'd shared with Mary at Alexandra's wedding with a longing smile.

He let go of the bar and landed with a plop in his waiting wheelchair—his special, no-choice buddy for the rest of his life—remembering the night of his sister's wedding.

Mary had changed at twenty-four. She'd become a woman who knew herself and how to tempt a man. She'd taken control of her life just like she'd promised the night of the prom, and she'd radiated confidence and inner peace because of it. Always reaching for that next step on his ladder to the pinnacle, Wes had wanted that. A taste of her secret recipe for contentment. She'd also happened to look amazing in the strapless maid-of-honor dress. It had been ice blue, he vividly recalled, enough to make him smile.

A forgotten sensation tickled down his spine until it reached the location of his spinal cord injury and stopped. He glanced out the window again, watching her sweep her tiny porch as he experienced phantom tingles in his toes. What was that about? Maybe he'd pulled something during his workout?

He'd always known Mary deserved a family of her making, a place to call home. A shot with a decent guy. He'd also had the wisdom to know that they were never meant to be together, so he'd never followed through on his "what if" thoughts. BP—before paraplegia. Useless, silly thoughts, meant only for thinking, savoring even, but never acting on. Until it was too late… AP—after paraplegia.

He wiped his face with the towel, searching the room for another form of man-against-machine torture to take his mind off these wandering thoughts. What was the point? He chose the cable machine, first lowering the sides of his specially made workout wheelchair, then grabbing the bar to begin a series of triceps cable extensions.

Was this how she lived now? Dragging her mini-house with her everywhere she went like a mega-sized backpack? What kind of vagabond life was that for a woman like Mary? She'd been raised in a trailer park by inattentive parents. He'd always pegged her as a girl who wanted to set down roots, who wanted a family more than anything else in the world, the kind she deserved, not the one she'd been born into. Though he could never picture a guy worthy of her, he'd still imagined her settling down, raising children. Now, apparently, she traveled the country alone. In that thing. A house suited more for a mouse.

The irony didn't take long to sink in about *him* wondering about what kind of life *she* led. *Take a look at yourself.* More money than one person could ever use, living alone in a fortress made of the latest building materials, a ten-million-dollar view of the Pacific Ocean out his front door, yet completely alone.

The last thing he needed to do was examine his own situation. Nope, he was determined to ignore that.

He shook his head. He wasn't ready to think about the AP future. Not after failing miserably when he'd tried to go back to work prematurely three months ago. How the humiliation had burned like a branding iron when his department head had suggested he'd come back too soon, telling him to take more time off to get a better handle on balancing his demanding job with being in a wheelchair.

His father's words to live by had infused his way of thinking. *Failure is not an option.*

The problem was, he already had. Failed. Big time.

He glanced out the window again, catching sight of the back of Mary as she pushed into her doll house.

One finger skimmed the area on his cheek where she'd bussed him when she'd first entered his house. He hadn't had the chance to dodge it. Oddly enough, her touch had produced a sweet warm feeling, as she always had for him, and had unleashed his wrath for catching him off guard, for daring to make him *feel* something. Because these days he, like his legs, refused to feel a thing, other than pain from working out too hard and too long. Which he believed was strength. As crazy as it seemed, physical pain reminded him he was still alive, not locked away by his own choice in this castle by the sea.

He guided his top-of-the-line workout wheelchair down the hall, past the specially built elevator to his bedroom, where he would have slammed the damn door if he could've only figured out how to get the right amount of leverage to do it.

This was his truth now. He was a guy stuck in a chair.

Mary went about the business of settling her home after another long journey. For the last two years and over a half-dozen moves, she'd lived in the tiny house she'd helped design and for which she'd paid cash. Another lesson she'd learned inadvertently from her parents.

She'd chosen to bring her house along with her wherever she got assigned, rather than stay in cold, short-term rentals or soulless extended-stay hotels. This was home. She'd carefully chosen the floor plan to meet her every need, yet using the smallest amount of space necessary. That had turned out to be two hundred and fifty square feet. She'd gone the woodsy cabin route, yet the repurposed materials they'd used to build the house were surprisingly light, making it easy to travel, as long as she was willing to drive a pickup truck. Which had cost nearly as much as the house!

Her living room space came complete with a large enough mounted flat-screen TV. The kitchen had been a bit trickier, yet she'd made it state-of-the-art enough to make do, since she enjoyed cooking. She'd settled for a two-burner gas stove, minimal counter space but with a built-in table that folded down and opened up when it was time to eat or if she needed a place to knead bread dough or cut out cookies. The half-sized refrigerator kept her eating fresher and healthier, since she didn't have much storage. Yes, the kitchen sink had to double up for face-washing and tooth-brushing, but for payoff she'd managed a nearly full-sized shower, with a stackable mini-washer/drier nearby and a petite toilet, all at the back of the ground-floor living space.

She chuckled, thinking of her mini-house as two stories, but her favorite spot in the entire tiny house was her loft bedroom. That counted as a story, didn't it? Plus, the permanent wood ladder she needed to climb to get to the loft doubled as a small A-framed bookcase downstairs. No space went to waste, and she liked living like that. Unlike the ratty tin and Formica filled trailer she'd been raised in, this was truly a home. Cozy. Warm. Filled with life. Her life.

She might not be able to stand up straight in her bedroom but, whichever city she set the house up in, each morning she could peer out of the small "second story" window at the head of her bed to greet the day. The view changed often, and so far she liked it that way. This time, she had the luxury of parking on Wesley's grand Malibu estate, and she was guaranteed to see the ocean first thing every sunrise. If she hadn't been so depressed about seeing him, she'd be excited about living here for the next two months. What she needed was a serious attitude adjustment.

She sat on the long pillowed and comfy couch, which doubled as a storage bench, with a cup of tea, and thought about Wesley. His situation broke her heart and she'd proved it with her meltdown on his doorstep earlier. He'd always been her hero, the guy with the world at his fingertips. The Prince of Westwood! *Invincible.* He'd made her want to be better than who she was, to build a dream then follow it to the end. Because of him, she'd pursued a doctorate after her post-graduate P.T. degree. She took a sip of hot black tea, thinking of his intelligent eyes, hers welling up again as her heart pinched.

The man might be considered disabled by everyday standards, but he was also a skilled neurosurgeon, and the world still *needed* him. She couldn't allow him to hide away in his gym day in and day out.

It seemed he had to relearn how to *be* himself. The confident, outgoing guy he used to be. That was a task far beyond her physical therapist's pay scale. All she could hope was for their once shared friendship and mutual respect to pull him back to what he'd been before the accident. Not the gym rat he'd become. Didn't he know that true strength came from inside, not from muscles?

Her phone rang. It was Alexandra. "How'd things go?"

"A little rocky at first, but he's agreed to let me stay for now."

"How does he look?"

Great! Sexy as ever. "Determined, and obviously buffer than I've ever seen him."

"If anyone can get through to him, I know you can."

"I'll do my best."

"Promise?" *Mommy! Mommy!* Mary heard children's voices in the background. With three kids, Alexandra never seemed to make it through a phone call without interruption.

"Promise."

"I'm going to have to cut things short."

"I understand. I'll keep you posted. Give those kids a hug from me, and two for Rosebud, okay?"

"Can you believe little Rose is one now?"

"Unreal." She'd missed her birthday from being out of state, but had seen videos, and had also had face time with her on the computer when little Rosebud had opened the gift she'd sent—a small rocking horse that talked to the rider. Rose had loved it and the grin on her face when she'd opened the package had managed to wrap around Mary's heart and change her life forever.

They hung up, and Mary remembered the day she'd first held Rose when she was less than a week old. The tiny bundle, completely helpless, had still managed to get her needs across with grunts and stretches, cries and flailing pink spindly arms. And the newborn had felt more amazing than anything Mary had ever held in her life.

Her education and traveling had kept her away from the births of Alexandra's first two children, Oliver and Bailey. But she'd been given the honor of becoming Rose's godmother so she couldn't very well miss out on meeting her right off. That meet and greet had changed her life.

A loving warmth fanned over her skin as she remembered how deeply she'd been moved by holding her goddaughter. How the tiny baby had reached into her heart and planted a need she'd never dared to dream of before.

As she stared out of the two decent-sized windows of her tiny home, looking out toward the beach, she thought of her own situation. She was at a crossroads in life and, at nearly thirty-four, she finally admitted what she really wanted. More than anything. A child.

It was little Rosebud's fault. And Matthew's, the sturdy little six-month-old she'd held just last week. Her patient, his mother, had been instructed to do some exercises and the baby had needed to be held. Mary had thought nothing of helping out until the sturdy boy with those chubby dimpled hands, two chins and a Buddha belly had looked into her eyes and squealed with joy. She'd never wanted to cuddle, squeeze and kiss a baby more in her life. Oh, yeah, she wanted one.

Now she dreamed of having a child. Illogical, yes, with no man in her life. Living completely without roots. An inconsistent job that took her all over the country. Yet she'd finally heeded the whisperings of her body that had been building for years, and with the recent help of two little ones, that whisper had turned into a scream. She wanted to be a mother more than anything. To have a baby all her own…before it was too late.

Finishing off her tea, she stood and walked the

few short feet to her kitchen sink. How exactly did a woman go about such a task on her own?

She glanced at the mansion up the walk, which may as well be a prison for its current purpose of shutting out the world for Wesley Van Allen, M.D. Then she put her yearning for a baby aside. Wes needed to be her first priority for now.

She was adamant about setting a time limit with him, though. Two months. Tops. She'd allowed for the lapse in a paying job into her annual budget for exactly that amount of time. If she intended to pursue her dream of having a child on her own, she'd need to change jobs to one where she could settle down in one place in order to be a stable parent. It was her chance to provide for her baby what she'd never had herself. Permanence, unconditional love, protection and opportunity. And, father or no father, she wanted it with all of her might.

She washed her teacup, deciding to take a walk on the gloriously beautiful beach. Maybe when she got back she'd crack open that bottle of wine she'd been saving, sit on her cozy front porch, have a toast to her latest post, and lift a glass to her future plans. Truth was, she could spend the entire evening daydreaming about becoming a mother, but…

Right now, her long-ago—but never forgotten—first crush had to come first.

CHAPTER TWO

THE NEXT MORNING, Rita met Mary at the door and escorted her as far as the stairs, which Mary took two at a time, priming herself for a fight when she reached the gym. Instead, she found Wesley dressed, freshly shaved, and with his hair tied up, waiting for her. Surprise.

"This is a change." She smiled, entering the workout room, but Wesley, dressed in a black T-shirt and grey sweatpants, didn't exactly return it. At least he didn't scowl.

"The sooner we get on with this, the sooner…" He stopped himself.

But she had a hunch what he'd planned on saying was, *the sooner you'll be gone.* "Two months. Remember? Give me two months and you'll be a different man."

Now came the deadpan stare. "I already am a different man."

She refused to take the bait. "You may be buffer than I ever remember, but there's more work to be done, though the outcome will be less obvious…" she held up her index finger "…but necessary." Without giving him a moment to protest, she grabbed a stool on wheels by the nearby wall in his top-of-the-line equipped gym and rolled over to his wheelchair. "I need to do a complete evaluation of your muscles and reflexes."

He pulled in his chin and his brows pushed down.

"You didn't think I was going to start you on exercises without first evaluating your motor and sensory status, did you?" From her large shoulder bag she pulled out a multi-paged form. "Let's get started."

"I've already been through this."

She'd learned from his online records—which she'd been approved to view—that he'd had sufficient occupational training for activities of daily living. She'd also learned about his past and personal medical history, which, to be honest, prior to the accident had been uneventful. But if there was any health issue, she'd leave that part up to his primary physician. He certainly seemed independent from the looks of him, all dressed and ready to go so early in the morning.

"Yes, but you haven't had a thorough examination in several months, and I need to compare your current status with the last one."

Her plan was to measure muscles, grade their power, tone and level of flaccidity. She'd test modalities of sensation, both superficial and deep, above his injury and compare them to the American Spinal Injury Impairment Scale. He'd nearly severed his spinal cord at T11-12, which made him paraplegic but able to sit on his own, which he obviously handled like the Prince of Westwood, and that definitely helped with breathing and the ability to deep cough. Both important for general health and well-being.

After the first part of the evaluation, which took a good half-hour, though impressed with his upper body strength and the fact he'd increased muscle mass since his last evaluation, she was most concerned about the decrease in the use of joints below his waist. With him being a doctor, she'd have thought he would have cared about such things, but she hadn't taken into account his mental outlook. He was an achiever and worked like the devil on what he could change, in his case developing strength and muscles like a regular Adonis, while ignoring the part he had zero control over—his hips and lower extremities.

She continued with her examination and as she used her hands to feel and measure his thighs, she sensed his discomfort and decided to lighten the mood. "Hey, it's not like you haven't had women groping and crawling all over you before, right?"

"They were usually naked."

He'd actually tried to make a joke—or a snide remark, but she preferred to think of it as a joke—and she couldn't let his effort lie flat so she played along. "Are you asking me to take off my clothes?"

She pinned Wesley's caramel eyes with her own, wondering where she'd gotten the nerve to be so bold, but rode it out in spite of her inner cringing. Acting this way felt completely wrong.

He didn't look away and it sent a subtle shudder right down her middle.

"That's a thought," he said, his voice a rough whisper that definitely wasn't snide.

She'd never pull something like this with a patient, and as long as she was here to help she'd expect nothing less from herself. "Excuse me, Wes. That was uncalled for. I apologize for crossing the line. You being an old friend shouldn't make a difference."

He didn't let her off the hook but studied her, his head tipped just so as he did. Inside, she squirmed, wishing she'd never pretended to be bold, waiting to see if she'd offended him and if he was going to let her have it.

"I'm still considering your first offer." His were now the eyes doing the pinning…and the teasing. The internal cringing doubled. He was testing her. She may as well be naked since she couldn't hide the total body goose-bumps.

"Gah! You win. I had no business acting all vampy with you. I'm the least sexy person on earth."

"Says who?"

"Oh, trust me, I am. Anyway, you win. I bow to your poker face." She went overboard, taking the ditzy route, hoping to keep him from realizing what she instantaneously had. He was paralyzed from the waist down. She felt safer with him. It was a sad truth she'd have to face herself with later in the mirror. She'd judged him without even realizing it, putting him in the "safe" male category, becoming gutsier as a result.

For that one instant, she understood how he must feel about the rest of the world judging him as a man. She'd inadvertently labeled him as less of a threat and had acted differently than she would've with any other male patient, simply because he was a friend sitting in a wheelchair. Inwardly, she shook her head. Ashamed.

He was an incredibly smart man, and intuitive, and, well, with friends like her, no wonder he'd become a recluse and an overachieving gym rat. Barbells didn't judge!

She took a deep breath and continued the examination using only the most impeccable professional skills from then onward.

And her heart broke again as she discovered

how stiff and nearly locked his hips, knees and ankle joints were. She had to get him back on track as this weakness would eventually impact on all the strength he'd developed above the waist. Not to mention his circulation and oxygen uptake. He might feel like "half" a man these days, but half of him was a lot, and the best parts, his brain and those strong shoulders and arms, would help keep the rest of him going. As long as he was willing. But he couldn't ignore the parts that didn't work.

She glanced at him. He still stared her down, keeping her feeling naked without a place to hide.

"So here's what I propose." She sat back on the rolling stool, and met him as close to knee to knee as she could get with his feet on the wheelchair footrests. "We work on a regimen to improve your lower body strength with passive range of motion exercises at first."

In response she got a blank stare.

"We need to preserve your joints—your hips, your knees, your ankles. Heaven forbid you should develop foot drop."

"Why?"

"For a better quality of life." That went over like a conk on the head. "You know that." More staring. "Or how about for when they finally figure out how to help paraplegics walk through nerve innervation." Still no response. "Come on, Wes, you're a neurosurgeon, you crack open people's heads for a living and do all kinds of things to their brains. Surely you've thought about the future, right?"

He shook his head. "These days I only think about the present." End of topic? Not if she could help it. Besides, she detected his defense mechanism in full force.

"Baloney. I believe there are hundreds of patients you've helped and saved who need you back on the job. I believe your future is still bright."

"Anyone ever tell you how annoying you are?"

Wesley was impressed with Mary's thoroughness, and also with her positive attitude, but wasn't about to let her know that. Why give her the upper hand? His personal doctor had promised him a much rosier recovery than he'd had, and as far as he was concerned he'd done his part to get as strong as possible. Yet he'd never get out of this damn wheelchair.

"I'm annoying?" She mocked surprise. "Yeah, all the time. I'm a physical therapist, what can I expect, I tick off all my patients. It's part of my strategy." Her expression went serious. "I know I'm bothering you, but I'm doing it because it's important. And speaking of important, where's your stationary bike?"

He screwed up his face. "In case you haven't noticed, I can't use my legs."

"You need the aerobic exercise to enhance circulation and increase oxygen. Let me show you." She dug into her shoulder bag and shoved a catalogue at him. "This is expensive, but from the looks of your house you can afford it."

He took a look, but wasn't the least bit enthusiastic about what he saw. The bicycle strapped the legs and feet in place and stimulated the muscles as the patient rode it, or so said the product description. *Completely high tech and necessary for paraplegics,* according to some Norwegian study.

"Since they did this study, I've recommended

this bike to all of my paraplegic and even quadriplegic patients."

He tossed her his best "so what" face, straight out of the teenage contrarian handbook. It didn't faze her.

"You might think it does all the work, but this little baby will keep you in tip-top shape." She stopped herself from saying more, but he understood she was about use the "D" word—"deteriorating", and take the broad-brush approach for life expectancy in paraplegics.

"Look, I get it, Mary. My tough-love doc showed me a video early on when all I wanted to do was shut down."

That notorious video, which he could tell from the change of expression on her face she knew of, used time-lapse photography to document a young man's demise. Hell, she probably carried around a copy of it in her bottomless shoulder bag, to use on uncooperative patients like him.

The patient in the video had been eighteen at the time of his skateboarding accident and had quickly given up on himself. The photographer had crunched ten years down to one minute.

The brutal video transformed a young generally healthy man into a shadow of his former self and had shocked the defeat right out of Wes. Mission accomplished. From that day on he'd worked at his rehab with a vengeance. Never wanting to quit, even when hospital personnel pleaded with him to slow down, he'd refused to give up. Since he'd been home, if the rehab PT didn't like his work ethic in the gym, he'd fire him or her. He didn't care which gender they were, out they'd go.

"So I don't have to paint that graphic picture for you, right?" Little Miss Sunshine returned.

"Right. I've seen it and I never want to go there." The thought terrified him; his worst fears had been laid out before him by that video. Never, ever, did he want to wind up like that. Not without a good fight.

"So I can order this for you, then? It says they can have a rush delivery here in a week to ten days."

The room went thick with silence as they carried out a staring contest. Why was she pushing this bike so hard? Did she have stock in the company, or know something he didn't?

She used her thumb and forefinger to pull back the hair above her forehead, a frustrated gesture, for sure. His stubbornness had gotten to her. "You're still a doctor, Wesley. It's completely possible for you to go back to being one *and* performing surgery again."

"Ha! That's rich." He let his honest reaction slip through the cracks. Been there, done that. Failed! Now he didn't believe a word. She may as well be selling snake oil. "I've already tried to go back to work and it was a miserable failure. My department head sent me home."

"Because it was too soon. How can someone as smart as you be so dense?" He saw determination in her eyes as she sat straighter, and he let the slur slide. Maybe he needed to listen to her. "As long as we keep your motor skills intact and your mind alert, there's nothing to stop you from going back when you're ready. The key phrase being 'when you're ready'."

Mary went back to her large bag, which apparently held the world in it from everything she kept taking out. She lifted a stack of medical journals and handed them to him. "Here. Why not catch up on the latest in neurosurgery?"

"Look, I appreciate your enthusiasm and concern, but I've got my own plan for getting back on the job."

"Sheer will and body sweat isn't a plan, Wes. My plan can't make you perfect again. No. But I guarantee it can and will help you improve and increase your chances of performing surgery again."

"How can you guarantee that?" He dug in, because he wanted what she preached so badly it hurt, but what if her promise never came to be? So far his Neanderthal work-out-until-you-drop approach hadn't panned out. Sure, he was buffer, but ready to go back to work? She was right. Not yet.

She pushed her face right up into his, those daring green eyes seeming to have X-ray vision over the battle going on inside his head. He tensed, shutting down a little, but he didn't look away.

"Prove me wrong." She put the journals on his lap. "Prove it. Give me a month and you'll see and feel the difference, then give me another month and you'll be amazed. I know it and totally believe it, and you'll just have to prove otherwise. Of course, all things considered, I'd rather you co-operated."

He couldn't deny the determination in her stare, or the genuine look of caring. She gave a damn. About him and his situation. And from the fire in her gaze, she wouldn't give up.

Then he felt it, that tiny flash of hope that throughout all of the trauma and disappointment and pain he'd suffered had refused to die. That pinpoint of faith in modern medicine and optimism for the future suddenly beamed brighter, because of *her* enthusiasm, and he found his mouth moving before he could stop it. "I doubt that I'll be amazed, but I'll take your challenge. Hopefully, you'll win."

Her eyes widened, she was obviously as surprised as he was, a sweet beam spreading across her face. She clapped her hands then pumped the air with a fist as if she'd just scored the winning point. "Yes! So does this mean I can order that stationary bike?"

"Order the damn bike," he said, rolling himself out of the gym.

* * *

The next morning Mary arrived with a mug of coffee, and found Wesley waiting for her in a halfway decent mood. She chose the stairs, two at a time once again, as he took the elevator to the second-floor gym.

"The first thing we need to do today is get you loosened up." She pointed to a thick floor mat beneath the workout bench. "Can you lower yourself to the floor?" She didn't have a clue how much he could or couldn't do for himself, so today would be one of discovery.

"Sure, but I don't make a habit of it."

"You should, you know. You have perfectly good arms, so I'm sure chair presses are a cinch for you."

"Let's find out."

She laced her fingers, stretched her arms and cracked her knuckles, then rolled her shoulders and stretched her neck side to side, like she'd be the one to do the lift and lower. He got a kick out of it, but didn't let her know. Then he put his hands on his locked chair wheels and pushed up until his hips left the seat. She stood back and let him move himself forward, repositioning his legs on his own, using his arm and shoulder muscles to their capacity as he lowered himself as close as possible to the mat and plopped down.

"Great," she said, helping him lie down and straightening his legs for passive range of motion. "Okay, you know what I'm going to do, right?"

He tipped his chin upward. "Yup." Reminding himself to be tolerant, that she wanted to help.

Positioning herself beside Wes, Mary took his right leg, carefully lifted and bent the knee and pressed the leg toward his chest, noticing how tight he felt. How long had he been ignoring the parts that didn't work? She ran him through several basic exercises to loosen his hips and knees and then concentrated on his ankles. He watched her intently as she repeated the same exercises on the other leg.

"Once I loosen your joints, I'll show you how to do all of this for yourself."

"Sounds like a plan."

"Yeah, so why haven't you been doing these?"

He shrugged, and she would have given anything to know what was going on inside his head.

It didn't make sense to work himself to the limit with weight training, then ignore the fragile part that needed equal attention. "Okay, I'm done here, for today anyway. You can get yourself back in that wheelchair, and we'll do your favorite part."

She sat back on her heels and watched with admiration as he bent his own knees then put the other arm on the wheelchair seat and essentially did a one-arm press to push himself back in. Impressive. And for someone who'd avoided doing this regularly, he made it look damn easy, too.

As they worked through Mary's planned program of weight exercises, Wesley was struck by how intent she was on balancing his training. She'd forced him to remember he had a lower half where circulation was just as important as the top. Where bad things could happen if he didn't take care of all of himself. Like a child, he'd been playing a game—*Maybe if I ignore it, it will go away.* One thing was sure as the sun, paraplegia didn't go away.

Halfway through the second set of butterfly presses with free weights, he focused away from himself, and watched Mary in all of her earnestness as she studied his technique like a perfectionist, adjusting his elbow here and his shoulder there. He liked the attention.

Later, when he shifted from his chair to the bench for some chest presses, Mary leaned over him, like a life coach, motivating him to keep pushing. He didn't need motivation, being determined as he was to be in top-notch shape so he could go back to work again—the upper half of him anyway—but he appreciated her interest and help. Which surprised him. All the other PTs had seemed like pains in the butt and he'd treated them all accordingly. But Mary was different.

"Let's up the weight," he said, testing her ability to let him call some shots.

"Sure." She put more weights on the bar and he went right back to work. Okay, so she was fine with him pushing himself.

In amusement, he watched her facial expressions mimic what he assumed were his as he lifted the heavier weight, and it made him lose concentration. He pressed the bar above his head, then laughed and lost ground. Spotting the weights, she had to move in quickly to catch the bar before it slammed onto his chest. Though he was perfectly capable of doing it himself, since he'd had to many times on his own, and had the bruises to prove it, he admitted he liked having her there, on point.

"You okay?"

"Fine. Just wondering when you turned into a slave driver."

"You're the one who wanted more weights."

"And you're the one who loaded them on." He got a kick out of goading her, and she fell for it every time. Just like she used to. And unlike the other PTs she was willing to push him as much as he wanted to go, not slow him down.

"So are you saying you want to take a break?"

"Could use some water."

She lunged for a bottle. "Five-minute break."

He gulped a drink. "I take it back. You're not a slave driver, more like a dominatrix."

"What?"

It felt good to tease and smile, like a lost and forgotten part of himself had suddenly shown up again. "All you need is some little leather get-up and a whip."

Her cheeks flushed and she stepped back. So he'd rattled her. Excellent.

"You'd look hot in skin-tight leather."

"Okay, the break's over. Finish your water, and let's move onto the back exercises."

Wesley caught her gaze. He'd definitely gotten to her. Good. "See what I mean?"

Her gaze shot up toward the ceiling, just like it used to do when she was a teenager and he'd frustrated and bothered her.

He pulled himself into a sitting position and she separated his legs on either side of the narrow bench with the weight bar just out of reach above his head. She straddled the bench in front of and facing him, and used her legs as support beside each of his knees, with her feet guarding his, keeping them in place.

"We'll start with fifty pounds, and go from there."

"What do you mean, 'we'? Seems like I'm doing all the lifting here."

"As you should be," she said, with a serious as hell expression.

She squeezed his shoulder and it took every

last bit of his attention away from the teasing. Her hand on his shoulder woke a bundle of nerve endings, and warmed the skin all the way up to his neck. He couldn't deny he'd missed the touch of a woman these past nine months.

Her touch made him think of the last time he'd seen her. It had been at his sister's wedding, where they'd played a dangerous game of getting high on bubbly champagne and acting like they didn't know what they were doing. Then they'd kissed, teasing each other with their lips and tongues, crossing the line with their touches. He glanced at her chest then quickly looked away, needing something to get his mind off those thoughts.

"So I'll do these exercises, but you're going to have to entertain me by bringing me up to date on your life." He didn't need her help to hold him in place on the bench. He balanced himself every day and used sand bags to keep his feet from straying, but he liked having her this close so he kept it to himself. Now he needed distraction from her nearness. "The last time I saw you, you'd just gotten your Master's degree. Oh, and your hair was a lot longer than it is now." Though he definitely liked this more cosmopolitan yet sexy look. He pulled down the weighted bar and did repetitions. Fifty pounds was nothing, but she'd find out soon enough.

She watched his every move, ready to jump in and catch him if he lost his balance. Again, unnecessary, but he'd let her do it since it probably made her feel useful.

"Well, I went on to get my PhD, then passed the boards and became a physical therapist."

"I get that part. I want the juicy bits. How many hearts did you break? Love affairs. The good stuff."

She gave a short laugh. "That'll take all of two minutes."

He raised a brow in mid-pull, hands spaced wide on the bar working the neck, shoulder and trapezius muscles. As always, it felt great. But her personal assessment of what he thought was a damn important part of a person's life—interactions with the opposite sex—felt all wrong. Two minutes? "I don't believe that for a second."

"I was totally focused on my career and it was hard to meet nice guys."

"So tell me about the rotten ones, then. Come on, I've been living in a cave. There must have been someone." He challenged her to dig deeper, just like she'd been doing to him. "I need some dirt."

She sighed, hands on her hips, her legs in a hip-wide stance. For a sex-starved man, even that looked sexy. He gripped the weight bar tighter.

"I got engaged when I was twenty-nine. I think it was more out of panic for my upcoming birthday. The first big one after twenty-one, you know?"

"Do women still let that bother them?"

"You do live in a cave. Wes, some things never change. Like right now, I'm almost thirty-four and I'm re-evaluating my life. If I wait too long, it might be too late."

"You don't look a day over thirty. In fact, I don't see much change at all since my sister's wedding and that's, what, ten years ago now?" He stopped in mid-press. "And too late for what?"

"My eggs are getting old."

"Eggs? Oh, for crying out loud, get a dog or

a bird or something. You can have a pet in that traveling house, can't you?"

"I could, I'm just not sure it would be fair to a dog or cat."

"A bird would be in a cage, what difference would it make?"

She shrugged, then stared off into the distance. That made him curious. "So why didn't you marry the guy you were engaged to? You could've had a bunch of kids by now."

Her prior open expression closed down. She paused. "It was the other way around. He decided not to marry me."

"That's harsh." Who in their right mind wouldn't want to marry Mary?

A wistful breath laugh escaped her lips. "Let's just say it took me by surprise." She kept staring toward the ocean, and he wished he hadn't picked at an old wound by being curious. "I guess he wasn't the one."

Wes wanted to guffaw at such a silly notion, but he could see she was still hurting, so he trod lightly. "You honestly think that? The 'one' bit? Hell, I figured that out after my first engagement."

With all of her attention now turned back on him, she'd clearly moved on and it relieved him. "How many times have you been engaged? Sheesh, Alex obviously didn't keep me in the loop."

Having successfully captured her interest, he sat straighter, ready to boast like the jaded man he'd become. "When I first graduated from medical school I thought I was in love. Didn't work out, though, when I caught her in bed with my roommate. Then, after Alexandra got married, I guess I was feeling a little pressure. I proposed to my girlfriend of the time, a fellow doctor, and we set a date. With my neurosurgery fellowship and her pursuing thoracic surgery, sometimes the relationship felt more like a competition. Anyway, we were both extremely busy and we wound up not having enough time for each other, and whatever we'd had going on before kind of fizzled out."

"Why didn't you bring her to Alexandra's wedding?"

Ah, so she hadn't forgotten their time together. Their second world-class kiss and more? To be honest, he'd purposely opted not to bring Giselle that weekend. When he'd found out that Mary was the maid of honor, and he'd also be in the wedding party, he'd wanted to go solo. He'd been planning to ask Giselle to marry him, but had put on the brakes at that point, deciding to wait until after he'd seen Mary again. He wasn't even sure why, but he knew for a fact that it was what he'd needed to do to be fair to Giselle.

"The wedding interfered with her schedule." Conveniently.

It felt weird, realizing how he'd intentionally set that up. No wonder his second engagement had been doomed from the start.

Quiet now, Mary directed Wesley into a new position and had him work one arm at a time with a dumbbell. As usual it burned and hurt, but in a good way. A challenging way that made him feel alive. Lately it was the only way he felt alive.

"So what was dumb schmuck's name?"

"Who?"

"Your ex-fiancé."

She laughed, obviously liking what he'd called her ex. "Charles. Chuck."

Now he guffawed. "Oh, hell, no. There's your proof right there. No way should you have married a guy named Chuck."

It made her smile and he was surprised how good that felt.

"What was your fiancée's name?"

"Giselle."

She made a funny face. "Of course your fiancée would be named something like Giselle."

Well, he had been a prince back then, according to his mother anyway. But he needed to bring the subject back to Mary. "You've got to have more to tell me about the last ten years than that." He strained out the words as he worked up a sweat. "By the way, Chuck rhymes with schmuck."

After he'd made her laugh, which again felt great, she set off telling him about the six places she'd lived in over the last two years, how she'd decided to design and commission someone to build her tiny home to her exact specifications. How she'd had to learn to drive a pickup truck, and how happy she was jumping from assignment to assignment, and loving the freedom of being completely self-sufficient. Yet he didn't believe for a minute that she was over her broken engagement with the guy with the unfortunate name.

Something else nagged at him. Her freedom. For the first time in weeks he focused on what he missed more than anything. The loss of his independence clawed at his chest and he nearly dropped the dumbbell.

“Woah! You okay?”

“I think I’ve had enough for today.”

Surprisingly, she understood, and didn’t push him. “You’ve done great. I can tell how hard you’ve worked over the past months. Once we get your lower extremity joints fine-tuned you’ll be feeling great. I promise.”

He zeroed in on those eyes that reflected the teal of the afternoon sea. “I’m going to hold you to it. Just so you know.”

“And I’d expect no less.”

Some twisted kind of mutual respect arced between them, until he got back on task. Once back in his wheelchair, he rolled himself toward the door. “Don’t let me down.”

"I won't, and that's why I'll be back later this afternoon to do more passive range of motion."

"Can't wait."

He'd suspected, like him, she'd only touched the surface of her life today. He'd skimmed his personal life so lightly she'd walk away not knowing an iota more about him. He wanted it that way, too. When he'd lost the life he'd taken for granted for almost thirty-seven years, he'd nearly given up. All that had gone before simply didn't matter anymore, because everything had changed. Sometimes it was too painful to remember what he'd lost. Sometimes he'd wake up in a panic at night, forgetting he couldn't use his legs anymore, freaking out while trying to get out of bed to use the bathroom. Then it would hit him. *I'm paralyzed.* He was living in the AP world now, he couldn't just get up and walk anywhere he wanted anymore. *After paraplegia*, everything had changed.

He used the towel she'd handed him on his way out to wipe down his face and arms, as always liking how exercising made him feel alive. Vital.

From the waist up.

He headed for his room and thought about Mary wearing those yoga pants with a midriff-showing workout top. Her body went in and out at all the right places, and he liked those curves. She had muscular legs, and not many women could boast deltoids, triceps and biceps on the arms like that, without coming off masculine. On her they were sexy.

Which brought him back to his unlikely ongoing attraction to the woman he'd always known had a crush on him. He'd taken that knowledge lightly back when he'd taken her for granted. Back then he wouldn't let himself explore the protective feelings he'd harbored for her, so he'd kept things superficial. What an egotist! Now, clearly, everything had flipped, and he felt edgy being around her, giving her carte blanche with his physical well-being. Hopeful, yet not knowing how much to expect in results. *Prove it, Mary. Please.*

Why had his mood taken a nosedive since seeing her again? Because she reminded him of everything he'd never have again? If that was the case, why had he started looking forward to spending time with her? Like right now, knowing she'd be back in a couple hours to push his legs to his chest. Something he'd been trained to do by himself months ago but had refused to keep up.

Nothing made sense since she'd popped back into his life. Before, he'd lived for his routine, worked like a fiend in the gym until exhausted, so he could sleep. And forget.

Now she was here and he'd started remembering. The problem was all he wanted to do was forget. What was the point in remembering?

It was too late. He lived in an AP world. Everything had changed.

So why was he still looking forward to passive ROM later today?

CHAPTER THREE

MARY ATE HOMEMADE granola with milk, preparing for another day of getting Wesley Van Allen back to where he should be. Physically, anyway. As she did so she sat on her front porch and took in the view of the thickly overcast morning and the sound of a cranky sea. Strangely, it calmed her.

Since spending so much time with Wesley the past week, she'd been inundated with memories of him at eighteen. The year she'd met him. Tall, tanned, athletic in a tennis player kind of way. Not nearly as buff as he was now, but he'd definitely looked fit. Hair nearly dark as midnight, with light brown eyes softening his otherwise commanding demeanor. Not your everyday brand of handsome. Back then he'd seemed so worldly and independent, so sure of himself. It had also been evident his parents had treated him like a prince. Alexandra had nicknamed him the Prince of Westwood and had snickered with Mary every time he proved it.

She could only imagine how shocking his becoming paraplegic had been to all of them, but most especially to a guy who'd never met a challenge he couldn't take on and win.

Was that why he'd agreed to give Mary two months? Because she'd stared into those unwavering eyes and dared him to?

Instead of graduating high school and heading off to university in another state, like most of his high-achieving friends, Wes had elected to attend U.C.L.A. Even though less than ten miles down the road from his West Los Angeles family house, he'd taken a dorm room, probably to feel some independence, but had still gone home every weekend. His mother had lavished attention on him, and his father had exuded paternal pride, feeding his princely calling. Neurosurgeon. Who'd want to move away from that? Alexandra had used to confide in Mary that she resented it. When she'd called after he'd first had his accident she'd sounded devastated and, more recently, desperate to help him.

Luckily for Mary—the teen who had seen Wesley as nothing less than a heartthrob—he had often been home for weeknight dinner. She'd kept her little secret from Alexandra, worried it could impact their friendship and she'd think Mary only came around because of him. Mary had loved Alex for accepting her for who she was. She'd found an amazing second home and hadn't wanted to risk losing it.

"Why eat cafeteria food when I have Sarah, the best cook in L.A., fixing dinner?" Wesley had once answered succinctly, when Mary had gotten up the nerve to strike up a conversation with him, using dinner as the "fascinating" topic, so flummoxed by his presence that it was the only subject she could think of. With her living in a trailer park, they'd shared so little of anything else.

Mary had never tasted such delicious food in her life before going to dinner at the Van Allens'. Her parents' idea of a home-cooked meal was a microwaved frozen dinner. If she was lucky that frozen meal hadn't started out with freezer burn. Eating at the Van Allens' had opened up a whole new world of culinary delights, and tastes she'd developed on her own all the years since.

She took another bite of the granola, which she'd baked in her own tiny oven until the honey glaze had been just right on the almonds and walnuts. She especially liked the addition of fresh coconut, now roasted to perfection and scattered throughout the nuts, seeds, and oats mixture. She'd definitely make this recipe again. Maybe she should take Wes some.

His attractiveness had improved with time, giving him character. She liked the hint of gray at his temples, and the fine lines accentuating his brown eyes. It seemed the high-stress workouts made them grow darker. Probably the hell-bound determination mixed with adrenaline was the reason for his dilated pupils.

When she managed to make him smile, which happened more and more often as they worked out together, she loved the grooves on either side of his mouth. She could tell an authentic smile, which brightened his entire face, from the obligatory ones that never reached those eyes. But most of all, since she'd first arrived a week ago, like boards getting ripped from a wall, their barriers had started to come down.

Yesterday he'd even invited her to watch a video with him, some crazy movie about an unlikely group of men and animals who guarded the galaxy. Who'd have thought he liked silly movies like that, and it had felt wonderful to laugh with him as they'd shared a bowl of popcorn. Also his suggestion. Had he always been an everyday guy, but she'd never noticed, or had his accident been the cause? And could she call a man stuck in a wheelchair for the rest of his life an everyday guy?

Her heart clutched hard over his situation, but she refused to let it bring her down. She'd treated patients in far worse situations, and she'd learned there was something special, a certain ingredient that made the difference between giving up or carrying on—and that component resided in the human spirit, something called hope. Medical reports said Wes would never walk again, but it didn't mean his life was over…just the life he'd always known. She didn't want to get dejected all over again about his current state, so she focused back on that silly movie they'd watched together yesterday. The popcorn. The laughs. And she smiled.

Mary thought hard. Had they ever laughed together when they were teenagers? Surely, if they had, she would have remembered how robust his laugh was, how it infected her and made her giggle right along. Once yesterday, while laughing, they'd glanced at each other. She'd tried to take a mental picture, because he'd looked like a man who didn't have a care in the world. Of course it wasn't true. Everything had changed. Still, there had been that moment. If she had to leave tomorrow, she'd carry that memory with her the rest of her days. That and the way he'd looked like an honest-to-God prince in a tux on the night of her prom when he'd told her he thought she was beautiful. And maybe that sexy dark gaze he'd unveiled after their hot make-out session at his sister's wedding reception. His pupils had definitely been dilated then, too.

Okay, she'd ventured too far down memory

lane, leaving her tensing her inner thighs. She checked her watch. Geez! She was running late. She crammed the last bite of cereal into her mouth, rushed inside and rinsed the bowl, then brushed her teeth at the same sink. Today she planned to up the repetitions—progress—and the thought made her smile.

Hmm, maybe she *was* a dominatrix in the making, but would one bring a client granola?

That was the second time she'd grinned that morning, thanks to Wesley Van Allen.

"You ever get lost in that thing you call a house, Harris?"

Two hours later, Wes gritted his teeth and spit out the words in mid chest press. She'd increased the usual weight by twenty-five pounds, and he handled it like nothing, even making small talk as he lifted and pressed. She liked it that he'd reverted to referring to her like he used to. *Harris.*

"It's plenty big enough, Wes. I have everything I need."

He glanced over, looked her up and down. "I

suppose living in workout clothes helps with closet space."

"I've got plenty of regular clothes."

"You can't tell me that if I invited you to Geoffrey's for dinner you'd have something special to wear."

"You mean glamorous? Does anyone even do glamorous anymore? Are we talking shoulder pads and glitter? Come on, we're in Malibu, isn't this the home of casual?"

"You've never been to Geoffrey's, have you?"

"Uh, no, but any woman worth her salt owns a little black dress, including me."

He stopped in mid-press. "Key word being 'little' with your living situation, I suppose." He smiled over his snappy reply.

"And when's the last time you went out to dinner?" She decided to press him on getting a normal routine. Why couldn't and shouldn't he go out to dinner?

"Is that dress sexy and does it show off your curves?" He'd obviously chosen to ignore her prodding him on living a more normal life, instead turning the conversation back on her.

She decided not to push it, and gave him a skeptical glance. "I've got curves? Since when?" She tried to brush off the topic, but he kept staring at her, making sure she knew he thought so. A whisper tickled through her with the promise of goose-bumps on the way, and there she was, tensing her inner thighs again.

"So tell me about your house." Thank goodness, he was letting her off the hook just as she had him, a moment before. Had he noticed her reaction? His eyes were back on the weights, his concentration on working his muscles.

And she liked what she saw popping up on his back and shoulders. "It's everything I ever wanted."

"I guess that means you never wanted much, huh?" This came through gritted teeth. So she *had* challenged him.

She playfully kicked his foot. "Come visit. You'll be surprised."

"I doubt my wheelchair would even fit inside."

"Of course it will. Hell, I'll even have Heath help me build a ramp. What time do you want to come?"

"You're serious, aren't you?"

"I'll even throw in dinner. That is if you tell me where a girl can grocery shop around here first. What do you say?"

She saw the battle ensuing in his thoughts, his troubled eyes giving him away. Of course he wouldn't accept her invitation, he was still too intent on punishing himself for the rest of his life for going water skiing and having an accident. Just like his father had insisted, he'd accepted it had been his fault. Well, to hell with that!

"Why not? Okay."

His surprising response stole some of the ire she'd worked up on behalf of his father. "Seriously, you'll come?"

"Sure."

Well, there you go. Now all she had to do was think of something spectacular to cook.

Seven o'clock sharp, Wesley made it up Heath's makeshift ramp to Mary's front porch in his ultralight sports chair. Small and compact, it was perfect for her house. He'd put on a pair of chinos and a button-down shirt for the first time since the accident. He'd been shocked at how loose fitting those chinos were since the last time he'd worn them, which had been before the accident. Earlier, he'd made a rash decision and used electric clippers to buzz cut his hair, military short. A Samurai topknot really wasn't his style. He ran a hand over his scalp, liking the fine prickly feel and the fact he'd let go of the confirmed recluse look.

Her door was open, and he had to admit that on first sight the lighting and wood-planked walls looked warm and inviting, though snug.

Her back was to him at the far end of the single room in the designated kitchen area, her hair was down and shining extra blonde under the soft glow of the indoor lights. Smooth jazz music played over speakers. She'd put on leggings and a gauzy sleeveless tunic top that billowed around the outline of her hips and upper thighs. She was literally barefoot in her kitchen, preparing dinner for him. Bohemian and sexy—not to mention showing off her toned and sexy arms—and he didn't need to feel from the waist down to notice that the sight of her turned him on.

Damn, it had been a mistake to come here. What was the point? A wave of claustrophobia swept over him at the thought of going inside, being stuck in his wheelchair. He clumsily attempted to turn around on the mini-porch before she noticed, so he could go back home and forget the whole thing. He'd call and say he'd developed leg spasms or something. He didn't fit in anymore and had already proved that by trying to go back to work three months ago. What a catastrophe.

"Hi! Come in. I'm so glad you came."

Hell, she'd caught him in mid-turn. He couldn't get out of it now.

"What'd you do to your hair?" Her smile was genuine and welcoming and his frontline, prepared-for-action defense cut him some slack. For that moment her appeal overcame his resistance. Maybe it had something to do with those dangly copper and gold earrings that sparkled and played peekaboo with her strawberry blonde hair.

"I figured since you're putting me through boot camp, I may as well do the military thing."

"Wow, what a difference."

You think? He hadn't bothered to look at himself closely in the mirror and was now curious. A buzz job was a buzz job, right? He rolled in front of a small mirror on her wall and took a look. Yeah, it was short all right. "Uh, thanks?"

"The grunge look was never your style."

True, he'd always taken pride in his appearance, but since the accident he hadn't given a flying whatever about the way he looked.

He saw her reflection standing behind him in the mirror. Right now her opinion mattered a lot, especially with her looking so damn good.

He turned. Rather than stare at each other, a million ideas winging through his brain, he rolled his chair around her, needing to distract where his thoughts were going and to fight off another surge of claustrophobia. "So show me around. Wait, I guess I've already seen everything."

"Ha ha. There are subtleties you've never imagined here, my friend. Let me point them out."

She showed him around a room that felt more spacious than its actual square footage, even with a whole lot of wood—knotty pine planks covering the walls, a peaked roof in the living room, laminate nearly black wood flooring. A Tyrolean mountain cabin on wheels. He noticed she'd rolled up a colorful area rug and tucked it by the wall, probably in preparation for his wheelchair. There were no less than four good-sized windows bringing in what was left of the daylight, which helped his subtle but unrelenting panic over the tiny space.

To break up all the wood, she'd hung a bright and busy oil painting on canvas above a pull-out desk, next to the bench covered in upholstered pillows. The couch? Okay, he'd buy that. A large-sized TV was mounted on the adjacent wall, and was currently turned to the jazzy saxophone and bass stuff, accompanied by a slideshow of beautiful nature pictures. *Not bad.* It helped smooth out his unease.

"Something smells great."

"Thanks. I found some free-range chicken cutlets at the Malibu Ranch Market. I'm trying a variation on chicken Parmigiana but with homemade pesto sauce instead of marinara. Oh, and since they had such a great assortment of wines, I chose a Pinot Grigio. Would you like some?"

Where were his manners? He'd shown up at her house without bringing anything, because he'd refused to think of this—being sociable with an old friend—as anything other than obligation. She'd challenged him. He'd taken the dare.

He'd had enough awkward encounters with old friends after he'd first had the accident. Everyone had tried really hard to act like everything was the same as always between them. Even his doctor friends. Except it wasn't. He sat in a wheelchair and couldn't pick up and do anything he wanted. Ever again. That had reminded each of his friends how much had changed between them, and had caused their visits to dwindle off. But this was Mary, not just an old friend but a physical therapist. She knew about people like him, treated him like she always had, and he felt bad about skipping a basic courtesy, like bringing wine or flowers when invited for dinner.

"So would you like some?"

Damn, he'd tuned out, a habit he'd gotten good at since the accident—going deep into his thoughts. "Oh. Yes, thanks." The old and forgotten part of his personality nudged him. "Sorry I didn't bring you any wine. I suppose the least I could do was bring dessert." It felt kind of good, too.

"Nonsense. I invited you. All I wanted was for you to come for dinner. See my place." She put the wine on a narrow counter beside the refrigerator and opened it. "To prove you'd fit."

"What's back there?" Curious, he pointed to a door frame with a sage-green burlap curtain. "Your pantry?"

"My bathroom and laundry room." She stepped aside so he could peek in.

Everything was smaller scale than normal, pushing down on him. Even the toilet wasn't the usual size, and there wasn't a sink. Tension made him clutch the armrests of his chair. The glass door on the positively one-person shower gave the room—if you could call it that since it was about the size of a normal pantry—a sense of being larger. Yet he still sensed heaviness with each breath in the tiny room. The stacked front-loading, stainless-steel washer and dryer couldn't have been more than a third of the normal size. More like Ken and Barbie-sized. What could he expect in a four-foot-by-four-foot area? But he could see for a single person on the road this would definitely do the trick, as long as Mary parked in a place with hook-ups for electricity and water. In other words, for a person who liked to go camping all the time. And definitely not for a person in a wheelchair.

"Compact, for sure, but surprisingly functional, I suppose." He scrambled for something positive to say.

"Absolutely." She opened the table lying flat against the wall, stabilized it with a latch, and placed their two wine glasses there. He rolled over and parked as she poured for both of them.

Taking another hint from his old sociable self, he offered a toast by lifting his glass. "Of all the strange places your travels have taken you, I'm surprised…" he tipped his head in acknowledgment of her efforts "…and pleased you arrived here. Cheers."

He took a sip, but she stood looking at him, dumbfounded. "You're glad I'm here?"

"Don't push it, Harris. Just take a drink."

She did, but smiled the whole time and he wondered how the wine kept from dribbling out the sides of her mouth.

As he took another drink, his eyes glanced upward to the loft. "Now, that's a bedroom sure to keep a guy like me away." The irony—both practical and sexual—struck him. Had his joke been tasteless or merely true and to the point?

She laughed good-naturedly, bearing with his crude-on-so-many-levels joke, then stepped forward and ran her hand over his head. It made him feel like a dog and he hated her for that for one second, until he saw the sweet tenderness in her peaceful green eyes. She'd meant no harm. It'd been a gesture of affection.

A word he refused to remember.

"With your upper body strength, you could probably take that ladder, or any ladder, without breaking a sweat."

He laughed, wondering if she'd just subtly come on to him. Hoping a little she had. "It's the getting down that will be the hard part." Yes, he'd intentionally skipped over the down and dirty bits on the loft mattress, knowing that probably wouldn't be part of his life again. Especially not with her. The previously fruity Pinot Grigio went sour on his tongue. "Don't you hit your head on the ceiling when you sit up?" Speaking of harsh reality.

"I used to, but I've adjusted now."

"You're nuts, you know that, right?"

"One person's *nuts* is another person's happy. I'm content here." She swirled the wine around in her glass and smiled at him.

He couldn't deny that she looked happy. "Even though it feels like a tree house?"

"Best damn tree house I've ever seen." She preened that silky hair with those earrings slipping in and out of view, and it hit him full on in the center of his chest.

Her happiness, her freedom, she nearly took his breath away. "One big gust of wind could have this place on its side." He deflected the feeling using one of his favorite defenses, being snarky.

"Look, I know it's small but, like I said, I have everything I need, and I'm happy here."

He glanced out the window up the driveway to his huge and lonely house. "That's more than I can say for myself so good on you. I'm happy for you." Why hold a grudge over his predicament against an innocent victim like Mary? She'd come to help him and as much as he'd wanted to kick her out at first, he was grateful she was here.

The oven timer went off and Mary rushed to take out the mouth-watering chicken, pesto and cheese scented meal from the toy-sized appliance.

Dinner was served and at first they sat in amicable silence as he savored the food, tasting pine-nut-flavored chicken in a way he hadn't enjoyed a meal in nine months. He'd turned half the lights off in his life since the accident, and Mary was insisting on being his generator. The light may be dimmer than it used to be, but it had become so much brighter than before she'd arrived. He needed to thank her properly one day soon.

Over dinner and more wine, him more than her, they opened up and talked about old times, carefully avoiding the most significant moments—their first kiss, a mind-blower—and their one date at her prom, the night he'd realized she was the most beautiful woman he'd ever seen, and had wanted her with everything he'd had. Not to mention the second life-altering kiss ten years later.

During the course of dinner, including seconds and followed by a spectacular apple crumble with vanilla ice cream for dessert, he felt human again—like a guy with feelings and passion and experience, and a surprisingly huge appetite. Nearly admitting that nostalgia was far better than isolation and bitterness.

His hands clutched the armrests on his wheelchair, remembering he'd never walk again. She'd almost tricked him into forgetting that detail.

He ground his molars and went quiet. Damn reality.

"Are you okay?"

"Sure." He hadn't fooled her. She homed in on his restless eyes, forcing him to meet her gaze. He needed to get out of there. The moment seemed like an eternity, which she made up for by crossing the short distance between them, leaning in and kissing his cheek. The exotic flowered scent in her hair nearly overpowered him.

"I know it must be unimaginably hard to deal with all you've had to, but I want you to know that you're the one guy in my entire life I'll always look up to. You're my life-changer. Nothing will ever alter that."

Moved by her words, maybe a little dumbstruck, he held her earnest stare, thankful for her honesty, unaware as she angled her lips on top of his, settling so gently before slipping away, leaving him craving more, more than he'd dared to want since he'd lost half of himself.

He left her house that evening scraped, bruised and frustrated emotionally, though his stomach was filled with good wine, food and dessert. On so many levels it had been torture, reminiscing about the past, knowing he'd never be that person again. That reality always managed to cut deep and suck the joy from a room, and it had happened so much faster in a treehouse-sized place like Mary's.

He'd enjoyed her company more than he'd cared to admit, but he wasn't that guy anymore. Her life-changer. He'd grown comfortable in withdrawing, it had become his default program, and he a computerized robot who only liked to work out in the gym. But Mary was making that escape route more and more difficult to navigate.

He'd been a complete gentleman when he'd left, not grabbing her shoulders and forcing her mouth to stay with his, as he'd wanted with all he had. Why not take what he wanted? He'd already lost everything else. But he'd chosen not to cross that line and had made a quick exit, so she'd never have a clue how torn up and mixed up he felt. Maybe he overrated his acting ability and she saw right through him—who knew?—but she'd seemed fine with his abrupt departure. He simply couldn't take another moment of what she offered—life, optimism, sexual desire. He'd let go of those feelings long ago.

Once home, after undressing and getting ready for bed, he remembered a promise. Mary had asked him to take ownership of his bedtime range of motion exercises, and he'd said he would. So he transferred from his chair to his bed and gathered his leg, bending the knee and pulling it toward his chest. It went so much easier than the last time he'd tried to do it a month or two ago. He had to give credit where credit was due, so he thought about Mary. Again. Probably a bad idea while lying on the bed after her tender kiss.

He'd acted like he thought she was crazy for choosing to live in a movable tiny house but, in truth, he'd gotten a kick out of her unusual living arrangement. Even envied her being able to pick up and move house wherever she took a job. The freedom. Independence. No strings attached.

He manually rotated his ankle around the socket, then flexed and pointed his foot, and thought how Mary had once been a caged bird living with those parents yet had always managed to be a free spirit. He'd admired that about her way back then, even though it'd forced him to take notice how much he depended on *his* parents. Had he ever been a free spirit? Why hadn't he chosen a university farther away from home when he'd had the chance, with several to choose from?

With his eyes closed, he grimaced. *Because of her.* Even then Mary had made an impact on his life. Sure, she was his sister's best friend, but she'd reached somewhere new inside him, a place that had never been touched, and he wanted to watch over her. Not in a big brother kind of way either. Hell, if he'd gone to Harvard, like his parents had wanted him to, he wouldn't have been there for her when Alexandra had sworn Mary needed a date for the prom. If he hadn't encouraged her to think big and go after her dreams, would she have had a different life altogether? She'd called him her life-changer—could it be true?

How could he ever know for sure?

His thoughts wouldn't let up and he suspected he wouldn't be getting much sleep tonight.

Over dinner, she'd told him all about her job with the medical agency, how she'd specifically chosen it in order to see the country. She could have made three times as much money signing on with a large hospital and staying put. Then she'd reminded him that, unlike him, her family had never, ever taken a vacation. She had a lot of territory to cover to make up for that. Staying put had never been an option.

These days, staying put was his only option. My, how things had flipped.

That was another thing he'd always admired

about her, she never complained about her lot in life. Nothing seemed to get her down. She'd been wise enough, even back then, to know that one day she'd be in charge of her own future, and since then, rather than blaming any failures on her parents, she'd done wonders with it.

He lay back and rolled to his side, adjusting the pillow under his neck, noticing that he could already sense the difference in hip rotation from consistently doing ROM.

There had always been something else he'd dug about her—she'd been crazy about him. Sure, it had just been a teenaged infatuation, and that usually faded over time. But somehow he'd known that, coming from Mary, even a crush could turn into forever. Back then he hadn't been anywhere ready for forever…but still the small one from the trailer park had called out to him. And then he'd kissed her.

Why hadn't he ever done anything about those instincts when he'd had the chance?

Adrenaline leaked into his chest, making his heart speed up and an anxious feeling spread like a flash flood throughout his upper body. The first kiss had knocked him for a loop, and *forever* hadn't seemed like such a bad idea at the time.

Bad idea. Really bad idea.

Fortunately, he'd come to his senses before he'd acted on his most basic of all instincts. He'd had big plans for his life, so had his father, and getting mixed up with his kid sister's friend couldn't be a part of it. Dear old Dad would have hit the ceiling if he had gotten involved with Mary. The man could only take charity so far.

He rolled to his other side, reaching down to adjust his legs again. Then he admitted something else—that first kiss had been for curiosity and had shaken him up, but in a good way; the kiss ten years later had been a test to see if his feelings had changed. The truth had shown up that evening at his sister's wedding—he'd never stopped wanting Mary.

But what the hell did any of that matter now, when everything else had changed?

Seeing her again, spending time with her every day, now that he was who he was, sometimes felt like rolling in ground glass. Yet being around

Mary was still worth it. He might never be the guy she'd look up to again, but he knew she still valued him, no matter what he'd become.

In the beginning, after the accident, he hadn't wanted to live anymore, but over time he'd found a reason to go on. He still loved his family and wanted to see them all have good lives, even though his father had been out of line insinuating he had been to blame for the accident. He had knowledge that a dozen years of medical training had taught him. Hell, he'd saved lives. Regularly! That had to account for something.

He'd discovered the gym and full-out body building. Well, upper body building, anyway. It had saved him and had given him false hope for getting back to work. He'd tried it his way before and it had backfired. He hadn't been ready to go back to work, mentally or physically. Having full-out leg spasms in front of a shocked patient had proved it. Now he had Mary in his corner, and even though she mixed him up with forgotten feelings, she was his one big hope to get back on the job.

Prove it, she'd challenged him, and he hoped with everything he had that he would.

She'd given him a second chance, and right about now that meant everything to him.

CHAPTER FOUR

MARY STARED AT the very close ceiling in her loft bedroom. She'd always felt cozy and protected up here, yet tonight she couldn't sleep. It definitely had something to do with spending the evening with Wesley Van Allen, and drinking wine. And what was up with the kiss?

Wes had looked rugged with that short haircut, and had seemed more his old self, and, well, she'd gotten carried away, once again proving his being in a wheelchair leveled the playing field in her head with a guy who'd always been out of her league.

Shame on her, but he was right there, easily accessible, and it had felt really great to kiss him. And she could tell he'd liked it, had seen the slight flare to his nostrils and a glint in his eyes afterward.

As hard as it was, putting thoughts of Wesley aside, she lay in the dark, staring at the ceiling and thinking about the topic that had captured her heart for the last year—having a baby.

She wanted a baby of her own so badly it hurt. She'd be turning thirty-four soon, and she couldn't exactly hold out for finding the right guy first. What if she never did? She wanted her own child to love and hold and cherish. She'd never felt cherished in her life, but she knew, after bonding with little Rose, it would be easy to do with a baby of her own. The older she got the more complications there could be with giving birth, too. Of course she'd love her baby, no matter what, but it would be challenging enough being a single, working mom. Why take any added chances by putting off what she could feasibly accomplish now? Maybe she should blame the urgent feelings about getting pregnant on all the Kegels she'd inadvertently been doing lately, thanks to Wes.

Which reminded her, she really needed to get going with her plans. Should she go with an insemination clinic or do it the old-fashioned way?

Ha-ha, with who? She squinted to avoid the image of a certain handsome man with a new haircut.

Not exactly putting yourself out there, are you, Harris? She could practically hear Wes's snarky retort, that was, if he had a clue what was on her mind. Then it hit her.

She sat bolt upright and conked her head on the loft ceiling. After seeing a burst of stars and rubbing out the pain, she lay back down but not before admitting her crazy idea might just work.

The bigger question was—would Wesley Van Allen consider being a sperm donor? Think of the phenomenal DNA! Smart. Handsome…so out of her league.

The idea was further proof she'd had too much wine to drink. Now with the bump on her forehead, at least she wouldn't feel a hangover.

Hitting her head had also knocked some sense into her. This crazy idea was asking too much, and Wes would throw her out of the house if she dared bring up the subject. Heck, he'd probably think she'd set up this whole *"Hello, I'm just pop-*

ping in to help you get back on track" for the sake of getting what she wanted.

How awful would that be! Even though it had honest-to-God never occurred to her about Wes until just now. He'd never believe her. She couldn't dare betray his trust.

She needed to drop it. Drop the subject right now.

She rolled onto her side with one tiny thought waving its hand far in the back of her mind. *Maybe?*

Wesley had been co-operative over the past few days since their dinner, but today's workout had seemed extra hard for him. Yet he'd kept pushing himself, getting frustrated when he didn't get the results he'd expected.

"Your head's not into it today. That's to be expected from time to time," Mary said.

"I feel like I've hit the wall." He dropped the free weights and they landed with a loud thud on the workout mat.

"Don't get discouraged."

He glared at her. "Don't give me that."

"Okay, you can keep pounding your head against a wall if you want. I'm just saying today might be a good rest day." She tossed him a towel.

He grabbed it and wiped his face, agitation tensing his eyes.

She drank some water, then offered him his own bottle.

He shook his head.

He wasn't about to be appeased. It was clear all he wanted to do, besides work himself too hard, was sulk.

"If you overdo it, you may regress. Take a break today. Watch some movies." *Why did she suddenly hope he'd ask her to join him?* "Get outside for some fresh air."

"I'll make my own decisions. Thanks." He made his point grudgingly.

She paced the gym, putting some distance between them. He'd seemed tenser the last few days of workouts since their dinner together, and she'd hoped he'd get over it, but he clearly hadn't. What a bonehead idea it'd been to kiss him. *Don't take all the blame, there could be dozens of things bothering him that I have no idea about.* But whatever was getting to him sure had a tight grip.

While standing behind him, she saw the incredibly fit man in the wheelchair gulp down the entire bottle of water. Everything he did lately was extreme. He tried too hard, expected too much of himself, insisted on pushing, pushing, pushing.

The guy needed an outlet beyond the gym. "I have an idea, why not use that beautiful Jacuzzi sitting out there on your patio, empty and lonely?"

He thought for a moment, his brows smoothing as he did. "That's not a half-bad idea. Maybe I do need a break."

She clapped. "Great."

"Come with me?"

"I thought you were sick of me."

"That's not the issue."

"What is it then?"

"Do you have to make such a big deal about everything? It was your idea, wasn't it? So come with me. That's all I'm saying." He spun his wheelchair toward the door. "I'll meet you out there in fifteen minutes."

"Deal!"

Twenty minutes later Mary showed up at the patio Jacuzzi. Wes was already in it, his arms outstretched along the tastefully patterned tile, the picture of a man of leisure without a care. From this vantage point, no one would know he needed a chair to get around.

She felt self-conscious taking off her bathing suit cover-up in front of him, because he didn't look away, just sat there grinning the whole time. It made her suck her stomach in tight and tense her inner thighs.

As quickly as possible, she slipped into the soothing water and sat across from him. Looking disappointed, he patted the spot beside him so she complied. He greeted her with a little splash, and she returned the favor. Smiling at each other, they settled down, submerged in the hot water, soaking in the sun and feeling completely relaxed.

"This feels great," she said, leaning her head back on the rim.

"I know. I should use this more often."

"I told you!" After a few seconds of silence she couldn't resist asking. "Why don't you?"

"It's not something I enjoy doing alone."

"Is it a safety issue?"

He shook his head, lapping up some water with his palm and dropping it on his head, wetting his face. "No. It's just with all these seats it's meant to be a group activity. Not solitary."

"True. But it's also therapeutic. Good for your circulation."

"Could you stop, just for one minute?" He lifted his hand out of the water to warn her. "Everything we do doesn't have to be about my rehabilitation. Can't we just sit here like a couple of old friends enjoying a soak?"

"I'm sorry, Wes, I wasn't aware that was how I came off."

"I get that you showed up to help me, but honestly, Harris, I've got it covered. Now that your wonder bike has arrived, everything is all set up. I've got everything I need."

"Are you saying my services are done here?"

"No." He scooted closer on the underwater bench they shared and whispered in the vicinity of her ear. "Start thinking of yourself as my guest."

"Not your dominatrix?"

He laughed, as she'd hoped he would. "If you want that job, it won't be in the gym." He winked, and she couldn't very well blame the warm water for the chill that ran along her spine. "Here's the deal. Things have been out of balance. Since you showed up, you've been running things. I get it that you want to help me, but I liked a lot about how I did things, too."

"You want more teamwork?"

"That's a start. I guess what I'm saying is we've got this time together, so why not enjoy ourselves?"

"Wow, this hot tub really has mellowed you."

He smiled, looking more relaxed than he'd been since she'd arrived two weeks ago. "Maybe we should do this more often."

Rita appeared with a tray of sandwiches and lemonade. "Thought you might like some lunch," was all she said, before putting everything on the nearby glass-topped table with an umbrella at the center, and heading back to the house.

"Thank you!" he called out, helping Mary understand he didn't take his ghost-like cook for granted. It meant more than he could realize.

The sky was cornflower blue, the water the perfect temperature, the buff guy next to her looked *hot* as hell, and he'd just invited her to think of herself as his guest. Could her day get any better?

She closed her eyes and sighed, and was quickly surprised by the arms that gathered her near, and the inviting mouth that landed on hers. Under other circumstances she would have tensed, but not here. Not now. Because everything felt too perfect. Especially the seductive kiss Wes had just planted on her.

Was this a dream? Making out in a hot tub with an even hotter guy? She opened her eyes just as Wes's fingers strayed from her shoulder and traced across her chest to the other side before he nuzzled her neck with more kisses. She hadn't thought it was possible to get goose-bumps in a Jacuzzi, but his touch had set off every last one of them.

"This was what was on my mind all morning."

"Kissing me in a spa pool?"

"Can you blame a guy for being grumpy?"

She stopped from asking if it had been a long time, since she knew chances were he hadn't ventured back into an intimate relationship with a woman since his accident. "Are you sure that's all that mood was about?"

His arms dropped from around her. She'd broken their "moment" and immediately regretted it.

"I focus too much on my condition, but I can handle it. Then here you are, doing the same thing. I've just felt under a microscope in the gym lately, and all I wanted to do was feel like a regular guy for a while."

"And here in the hot tub we can do that?"

"I'm just a guy sitting in a spa with a good-looking lady, enjoying myself." He splashed her full on in the face.

She squealed but retaliated, pushing water his way with both hands.

He laughed and doubled down, covering her with water, and she fought back. Soon they tired of acting like unsupervised kids and settled down, though still laughing. And damn if it didn't feel great.

"I'm hungry," he said.

"Me too." She climbed out and found two large towels draped across a lounge chair. She tied one around herself and before she could bring one to Wes, he'd already gotten himself out of the tub and was sitting along the edge of the small pool.

"Can you bring my wheelchair?"

She looked around and saw it subtly tucked away under the cabana and brought it to him, first spreading the towel on the seat cushion, with the sides open and waiting to cover him. With ease and muscle he hoisted himself into the chair. Soon they were sitting at the table under the umbrella, enjoying sandwiches and fresh lemonade.

She wasn't sure what had just happened back in that spa, but was really glad they'd taken the afternoon off. He'd gently reprimanded her for being too focused on his condition instead of seeing him as a whole person exactly as he was. She'd just had a good glimpse of that guy, too, and really liked what she'd seen. The trick would be keeping the balance from here on out.

Why did she suddenly feel like she walked a tightrope over her profession and her true feelings?

After lunch they went their separate ways, saying nothing about their shared world-class kiss in the hot tub earlier.

The next morning Mary showed up in the gym to find an even grumpier Wesley.

"I thought we'd just work out alongside each other today," she said in response to his unspoken gloom. "Is that okay with you?"

He harrumphed.

She'd thought long and hard about what he'd told her yesterday about not wanting everything to focus on him. She'd realized how he must have seen things, her showing up out of nowhere, sweeping into his life to, what, save him?

The idea made her cringe. "Hey," she said.

He pressed a huge amount of weights in response.

"Everything okay?"

He grunted.

Then it hit her. She'd spent a fair amount of time thinking about the issue between them last night—the unspoken attraction that was definitely still there—especially after their wonderful kisses shared in that Jacuzzi. "You know what this is about, right?"

"What what's about?" he said, after dropping the pulley weights and making a loud clank when metal hit metal.

He looked at her as if she'd become a talking mutant. Like she'd dared to read his mind and she'd better not get it wrong. Not a sound passed between them for several seconds as she got up the guts to hit him with the elephant in the room.

"Sex. This is about sex."

He continued to glower, squinting for emphasis.

"You miss it. You need it."

"For flipping hell's sake, get off my back."

Whammo!

His brush-off only made her dig in her heels. "I'm not the one pushing myself within an inch of my life. You're obviously trying to work off your pent-up sexual energy, and you've failed…"

If he could have exterminated her with the white-hot anger flashing in his eyes, she'd be toast.

"Miserably." She wouldn't back down. He needed to hear the truth and get some facts. Now was as good a time as any, plus it might break him of needing to overwork himself.

"Thanks for reminding me, Harris," he said, putting a dreadful emphasis on *Harris.*

It hurt to see him focus his anger on her, yet she refused to break eye contact. "You can have normal sex."

He went still, seething, nearly fitful, clearly using every ounce of restraint to keep from verbally attacking her. "In case you haven't noticed, there isn't anything that's normal about me anymore." He'd lowered his voice, yet every word shouted, *This is a warning. Back off!*

She opted not to listen to the unspoken message. "You're a neurosurgeon. You know it's possible. Just not the way it was before."

The fire in his glare showered her with restrained anger, making her face go hot.

"Then what's the point?"

The rush of exasperation hit her by surprise. She was a professional, had had this conversation with several male patients over the years, yet Wes had gotten to her. He'd won. Shut her down. For now she'd give up on the topic. She picked some free weights and went to town with curls. "You'd be surprised."

He rolled the chair toward her, challenging. This conversation was far from over. "What do you mean?"

Oh, hell, was he thinking she'd just made him an offer? That wasn't her intention at all, it was the subject that needed defending, not her talking specifics. What should she say?

Act professionally. "There are many wonderful women around the world who are devoted partners of paraplegics."

Though buffer and stronger than he'd ever been in his life, he was still fragile. "You know I've always had a crush on you, Wes, and no matter how you are now, that hasn't changed. Your wheelchair doesn't factor into the equation. At all. You're an impressive and appealing man."

Emotions ruled his thinking. Now he'd gone

from red-hot anger to sizzling need in record time. Very moved by what Mary had just said, Wesley took her hand, pulled her down to his eye level and, letting the barrage of desire take over, he kissed her. He forgot about where he sat or why they'd been spending so much time together over the last few days. All he saw was a woman he'd never gotten out of his mind, who'd just admitted she still had feelings for him. And he went for it.

As they kissed, every obstacle in his head stepped aside. He freely explored the lips he'd reacquainted himself with yesterday in the hot tub. He did what he wanted, took what he wanted, and she met his rough kisses with sweet music in her throat. Her reaction turned him on even more. As his tongue slid over the velvet of her lips and inside her mouth, he remembered what it was like to be a man.

She'd ignited fire inside him, and the heat of it, after all this dormant time, shocked him. "Prove it," he said over her mouth, mid-kiss. A moment later he stared into her fully dilated pupils, cluing him in she'd been as much into that kiss as he'd been. "Prove that I can still have sex."

Wes's dare sent a disturbing chill down Mary's spine. Shaken back to consciousness, she pulled away, fully aware of his clutch on her arms. He'd laid down the gauntlet, challenged her, and she was nowhere ready to prove anything!

She stood, but his hands went to her waist, keeping her near, staring at her like the commanding man he'd always been.

It took everything she had to stare deeply into his hungry eyes. She saw raw need there—*Help me be whole again.* He needed her help and, to be honest, with her recent craving to have a baby, she needed his. The next thought sent a lightning-bolt reaction through the center of her chest. Could they strike a bargain?

Her stomach twisted at the possibility. That would be all wrong.

And completely unprofessional.

She gingerly pushed back from his grasp, which had slipped to her hips, frantically thinking of a way to smooth over this huge shift in power. In the course of a minute of hot and heavenly kisses, she'd managed to annihilate all the trust she'd worked so hard to build in Wes. He'd found out her weakness, and now she had to take back her role as physical therapist. "I think we both know that would be a huge mistake."

"Was yesterday and the day before a mistake, too?"

"I'm sorry if I gave you mixed messages. I have such fond memories for you, and it was so nice to have you in my house, and yesterday in the hot tub…I overstepped my bounds. I'm sorry." Oh, God, would he buy it? It was partially true.

"*Fond. Nice.* Such tepid words. That's not what I felt yesterday or just now."

She swallowed the dry lump that had lodged in her throat. "Look, I felt what you felt, but that doesn't matter." She forced herself to stop wringing her hands. "I came here as a friend, to help you get back…" Oh, damn, her fingers kept interlocking and unlacing, and here she was about to stumble over her words.

"On my feet?"

His transparent fury cut deep, and hurt to the

point of knocking the air from her. In a few short seconds everything had fallen apart. She had to fix this, and it was time for her to plead. "You know that's not what I meant." Regret washed over her in bucketfuls, throwing his own sentence back at him, but she couldn't figure out how to make things right. How to keep things in balance. Because her mind had been jumbled by that kiss.

With muscles twitching on both sides of his jaw, he made a jerky movement and rolled his wheelchair away. "I'm taking the morning off. Doctor's orders."

Mary decided she had blown it big time. She jogged along the beach, her toes digging little holes into the wet sand, thinking she should probably pack up and leave. An overcast day, it seemed to accentuate the scent of seaweed, and the downcast mood that had overtaken her. Unintentionally, she'd humiliated Wesley, a man whose pride had always ruled the day. A man who now sat in a wheelchair, and who'd somehow gotten up the nerve to ask her to have sex with him.

As she ran, the rhythmic sound of waves crashing tons of water onto the shore helped her calm down. Everything seemed mixed up. She'd never encountered this kind of problem with a patient before. Because they had a history, being around him had forced her to realize she still harbored feelings for him. The moist air soothed the tension that had built up in her throat.

The crazy thing was, her wish to have a baby and have Wesley donate the sperm had planted itself in her head and wouldn't go away. She needed to shake it out, because he wouldn't even talk to her now, let alone offer to donate sperm.

Every time she looked at him from now on, she'd know his thoughts, because he'd asked her to prove he could have sex again! It had to take a lot of nerve to ask it, and she'd brushed his wish aside, humiliating him further.

The scariest part of all was how much she wanted to go for it, as in, with all of her heart! There was no way she could discuss her proposition with him. If she didn't word things perfectly, he could feel used. So would she. That could make a wonderful thing seem icky. No, she needed more time to work things out.

Who knew how long he'd go back to being a hermit after their blow-up?

Should she leave? Had she blown it that much?

Her cellphone rang and she saw it was Alexandra. "Just checking in to see how things are going."

"They've been going pretty well, but today was bad."

"Don't let him bully you, Mary. He's done it with every person we've had work with him."

She wanted to say it was more than that, that she'd had a lot to do with the problem. And she wasn't sure she could fix things. "It's not that easy, Alex."

"Please? Oh, I'm begging you. Don't give up on him. He may not act like it, but he needs you, Mary. Please."

How could she let down the person—her first best friend—who'd always accepted her as she was and had changed the course of her life by bringing her into her home? "No need to beg,

Alex. I said I'd come for two months, and I promise to stick it out."

She hadn't come here as a physical therapist—she'd come as a friend first. He never would have tolerated her staying around if they hadn't had that connection. She'd played with fire by kissing him, now she had to deal with the consequences. He wanted her to prove that he could have sex and enjoy it with a woman. A really big deal to every man. No, it wouldn't be exactly the way he'd experienced sex before, but from all the reports and studies she'd read, it would definitely be satisfying. Just different.

Her strides got longer, her breathing harder. She pushed aside her desire to ask him to consider being her sperm donor to not confuse things between them any further. Yes, she was here as a friend, but she needed to step up on the PT side and help Wes return to a full and fulfilling life. Getting him strong enough to go back to work. Enhancing his dexterity so he could perform surgery again. His rehabilitation was reason enough to sacrifice her secret wish.

As for sex, well, she had another idea, but first

she needed to get in touch with one of her prior patients. Soon. She'd been here just shy of three weeks, she knew her menstrual cycle, and time was running out. Great, just what she needed, to put more pressure on herself.

She'd run herself ragged on the beach, which had been her plan. Now she'd shower and crash in her house for the rest of the afternoon. If she were lucky, she might actually have some clear thoughts. But when she reached her door she saw a note tucked in the seam.

It was from Wes.

Have dinner with me. Since you won't accept a salary from me, the least I can do is feed you.
W.

This had to be his way of apologizing, yet she wasn't ready to face him again. Not before she'd done more research. She opted to skip the shower. She'd also call Rita, not Wes, since she presumed she'd be the one to cook dinner. She'd tell her she couldn't make it tonight.

Coward's way out, yes, but it would serve her purpose. She had to get things back on track between them.

Two hours later, after a thirty-minute conversation with her former patient, Sean, the busiest bachelor in a wheelchair she knew, her laptop was open to the ultimate guide to dating paraplegics. While deep into research on products, there was a tap at her door.

Still in jogging shorts and tank top, her hair a mess, through the window in the door she saw the outline of a man in a wheelchair. Wes.

She jumped up and opened it, recognizing that look of chagrin, and because of his humble attempt to make things right by inviting her to dinner earlier, she was more than ready to forgive him for pressing things earlier.

"Are you not having dinner with me because you're still mad at me?"

"Hi. No, actually I'm working."

"But you're still upset."

"I took a long run and fixed that."

He glanced over his shoulder. "I haven't been down to the beach in a long time. Had Heath build an access for me ages ago, but have rarely used it."

"That's a shame."

"Take a walk with me?"

He'd come in his sports chair, light and maneuverable, clearly ready for the packed-down sand on the beach at low tide. Considering how messed up things had been earlier between them, and the fact the man came all this way to ask her for a walk, how could she refuse?

"Let me put my shoes on."

Twenty minutes later, they'd spoken minimal words, choosing to enjoy the gorgeous ocean, the light pale tone of evening after the sun had set, taking the burst of bright colors with it. Cruising along with the tide in the twilight, she sensed a softening in him. He hadn't come to apologize or to prove anything, he'd come to…come to what? To court her?

"So, I guess I shouldn't have expected you to have dinner with me after my outrageous request earlier."

"You certainly surprised me." Yet she understood how much he needed to prove. How much that meant to his personal identity.

"I'm sorry."

"No need."

"I was out of line."

"Okay, apology accepted." She shrugged. Hell, she knew firsthand the need to prove something just out of her reach. Since that moment of holding newborn Rose when she'd been hit with the deep unwavering need, with all of her heart and every other part of her, she wanted to be a mother. A most basic function for a woman, and something she couldn't do by herself. Of course she knew how he must feel about a man's most basic function—sex—so she'd cut him some slack for pushing a topic neither was really ready for.

"So I was thinking how much I enjoyed having dinner at your house, and thought we should take meals together. All I do is watch the news and get indigestion. It would be nice to have someone to talk to."

"Or, in our case, to argue with?"

That got a good-natured laugh out of him, and it touched her more than she'd expected. He was really reaching out to her, and she needed to be careful not to hurt him.

“That, too.”

“I’d really like that, Wes. I get bored eating alone every night.”

“Great. Tomorrow I’ll fix you my go-to meal.”

“Let me guess, it’s the one great thing you know how to cook to please the ladies?”

“Nah, I always have Rita fix those meals.”

It was her turn to laugh, and it felt good to let go of all the tension between them.

They’d started back toward the house since it was quickly growing dark. Though Heath had thought of everything, lining the long wooden path from Wesley’s yard to the beach with solar lights. It looked like a mini version of an airport runway.

“Now I’m really intrigued what that dinner will be.”

“You’ll have to show up to find out.” He took her hand and tugged her close, then put his hands on her waist. “Come here.”

She sat on his lap, wrapping her arms loosely around his neck. Eye to eye under the moon, his were dangerously dark. He lifted his chin and they kissed, natural as breathing. He kissed her well, but didn't linger for more. Just a simple kiss good-night. But nothing was simple with Wesley Van Allen, and she felt that kiss all the way down to her toes.

He rolled the chair with her on his lap for the last few feet on the wooden planks. She took a deep breath, enjoying the ride, glancing up in time to see a shooting star. "Look!"

He saw it too. "Too bad you won't be here in August during the Perseid meteor showers. They put on a great show."

It hit her then that their time together was limited, and as light and airy as she'd felt a single moment ago, the sudden weight of leaving Wes was like a punch in the gut.

They'd made it all the way back to her tiny house in silence, and rather than take the ramp up, Wesley stayed put, so she got off his lap and strolled to her porch.

"I'll see you at eight tomorrow morning," she said, leaning against the rails. "I've got some new things to show you."

"Now *I'm* intrigued." As darkness settled, all she could see was the silhouette of his body and head and the white of his teeth. "It had better not be more rehab exercises."

She smiled in his direction. "You'll just have to show up to find out."

"You're a tease, Harris," he said, turning his wheelchair and heading back toward his house. Leaving her wondering if that had been an intentional *double entendre*. "By the way," he said over his shoulder, "I've been doing some research myself and have something to share."

"Really?"

"Yeah, you'll just have to show up to find out." He kept rolling.

"Who's calling who a tease?" she called after him.

That night Mary made a huge mistake and let her mind wander. She imagined what it would be like to become Wesley's lover. After the kisses they'd been sharing, the way her body had come alive around him, those sensations were fresh in her mind.

The bittersweet thought was supposed to be positive and uplifting, but knowing she'd be leaving in a little over a month, it left her with mixed emotions. She tossed and turned in bed.

Besides sex, there was another gap in his life. A huge one. He was a specially trained doctor, who needed to work again.

Rushing to sit up, this time she stopped short to avoid hitting her head. Her laptop was on the mini dresser—a former regular dresser that had had the legs shortened to fit the loft A-frame space—so she reached over and grabbed it then sat in the center of her bed, the one spot where she could sit straight. Booting up the computer, she surfed to an occupational therapy website that promised to enhance digital dexterity, something a guy only pumping iron for the last nine months may have lost.

In order to feel whole, Wesley needed two things—neither of which was his legs—one: to be gainfully employed again, and, two: a gratifying sex life.

Yeah, she certainly had her work cut out for her before she left.

CHAPTER FIVE

THE NEXT MORNING, Wesley detected an extra sparkle in Mary's eye when she showed up in the gym. He hoped it had something to do with all the kisses they'd been sharing, but he was on task and didn't wait to find out.

"Let's skip the gym exercises for now, okay?" he said. "I've got some things I want to show you."

That totally captured her interest and, instead of disappearing, the sparkle brightened. "Such as?"

"Get out your laptop."

She pushed a small table toward his wheelchair, then brought a chair to sit on. Digging into that overgrown shoulder bag, she dug out her laptop.

"I want you to have a look at this." He took charge, booting it up, and soon clicked on the video he'd discovered about a doctor who'd become a paraplegic and designed a special wheelchair so he could continue to perform surgeries. The accompanying article showed how the electric wheelchair could elevate to a standing position with support around the chest and on the legs above and below the knees.

Mary studied the contraption carefully.

"I wondered how healthy it might be, staying in that position for long hours performing brain surgery. How it might affect my breathing and circulation. But the idea of being able to do procedures is a game changer." For emphasis, he played a short video with the guy doing an orthopedic procedure.

"Amazing what someone can do with motivation," she said.

He took it as though she'd just questioned his, and immediately got defensive. "I went back to work too soon, there wasn't a contraption on the earth that could've helped me." He'd had the misfortune of running into Giselle his first day back and what he'd seen in her eyes hadn't been sympathy but pity. She'd wanted to help push him down the hospital corridor, and he'd hated her for it. He'd miscalculated so many things about returning to work, like leg spasms and patients caring more about his condition than their own. Even the logistics of performing a simple examination had tripped him up.

The week-long experience had been humiliating and he'd never felt that way in his life before. He'd hated every second of it, had gone home and never wanted to open his door to the outside world again. Good thing he was a guy who got bored with wallowing quickly, and buried his feelings behind barbells and weight machines.

"Wow. With something like this, nothing can stop you from picking up your career and carrying on with your life."

He understood why she held him accountable for his future, it really was all up to him. Her belief in him felt hopeful, and he was grateful for that, so he smiled. "I know."

"And we're on the same page!" Instead of gloating, which he'd expected her to do, she reached back into her bag of goodies and produced a deck of cards. For some crazy reason her doing something so off the wall tickled him, but he donned a poker face until he could figure out where she was going with the prop.

"We've been working your large muscles but overlooking your fine motor skills. So here's the deal; if you want to go back to doing surgery, which after seeing that video I know you can do, you need to start working on your fingers and hands."

Would she stop at nothing to get him back to work? At a loss for how to respond, he let his mouth drop open.

She moved her laptop and edged the deck toward him. "So shut up and deal."

After he'd gone back to work too soon, and couldn't even handle seeing patients, he hadn't let himself think about ever performing surgery again, especially neurosurgery, which often required hours in the OR, and total focus on fine details, often so minute it required special headgear with magnifying glasses. One false move and someone's life could be changed forever. He'd never been too confident to forget that, but these days, sitting in a wheelchair, he found it much harder to wrap his brain around. Yet his finding the video of the standing wheelchair opened up his world and proved there was something out there to accommodate his logistical problem. He could stand upright in the OR again. And potentially perform neurosurgery! All he had to do was order one.

For an instant, he was overcome with fear, but he fought it off and instead focused on the pretty lady holding out some cards.

He dutifully took the deck, shuffled and dealt, soon realizing, if push came to shove, he'd never qualify for a job as a dealer in Las Vegas.

"Try it again, but faster," she said.

Like a character actor, he needed motivation. "What game am I dealing for? And don't say, 'Go fish'."

She made a cute thinking face, glancing toward the ceiling, distracting him and ruining any chance of his impressing her with his dexterity skills.

"How about gin rummy? Ten cards."

Fair enough. He could handle ten measly cards, so he dealt.

"Again," she said, ripping away the deck—along with his instant of pride for counting out the right number of cards in what he considered a reasonable span of time—tidying the stack and handing it back to him.

Again and again he shuffled, not making much progress on the speed. But he tried, in a sorry sophomoric attempt to impress her. "Are we ever actually going to play this game?"

"Keep dealing." Total dominatrix. And he liked it.

After a few more deals she gathered the cards and put them away.

"Not good enough?"

"Not bad, but there's more to do."

The day was sure to go downhill from here. He fought the urge to make the sign for loser and posting it on his forehead. *Failed at card dealing.* Still, it amused him.

She didn't give him a chance to think for long before she produced something else from that huge bag of hers—a quarter. "Can you roll a quarter through your fingers?"

"Wait. We're through playing cards? I was just getting the hang of it."

She ignored his taunt. "The quarter roll. Ever tried it?"

"Never." He had to admit he'd started liking her bossiness, but only because she looked so cute doing it.

She handed him the coin, then opened the laptop again. "Watch this little video first."

She brought up a well-known video site and a tutorial on coin rolling. Tricks. She'd sunk to teaching him common sleight of hand tricks. But he liked her undivided attention, so he co-operated.

"If I do this, you have to kiss me."

"The joy of victory isn't enough?"

"Not for me. I need some lips." He pointed to his mouth. "Yours. Right here."

Her devilish angel expression nearly knocked him out of his chair. Now he really needed to kiss her.

"You're on." She tipped her head. "Make that quarter roll."

He positioned the coin just below his knuckles

on the back of his hand and tried rolling it, using each preceding finger to prod it along like the video had shown. Slow but steady, with Mary's encouragement, he attempted the task without complete success. But he wouldn't give up. She'd laid down the gauntlet, in this case a quarter, he'd bargained for a kiss, and he was damned if he'd fail. A half-hour later, he finally perfectly advanced the coin from finger to finger on his right hand. Yes!

She applauded, but the big bonus was her smile. It made him stop and take it all in, bright, beautiful and sweet, and he called in the kiss. She willingly obliged, taking her place on his lap first. He glanced into her eyes, enjoying the little thrill, knowing she was about to kiss him, and let her deliver the kiss her way.

She was definitely out to impress, planting her hands on either side of his face and her mouth soft and warm over his. He tried to hold back but couldn't. Every kiss they'd shared had only made him want more and more of her. Their tongues soon found each other's and just on the verge of deepening their kiss she was done.

"Now do it on the left side." Back to that seductive impish expression, and him definitely wanting to kiss her again. He did what he was told, but not before bargaining for more.

"And if I do, you have to kiss me again, but this time I get to use my hands."

"This is starting to sound like a new kind of strip poker."

"I'm hoping for a lap dance."

She sputtered a laugh. "You'd be so disappointed."

"I doubt that."

"I don't have a vampy bone in my body."

"Now I know you're lying."

With Mary still sitting on his lap, he stared into her darkening green eyes, liking the desire buzzing beneath his skin. She'd been bringing him back to life step by step since showing up on his doorstep. He thought about kissing her again, but had waited too long since she scooted off his lap and stood, handing him back the quarter.

Since the left was his non-dominant side, it took thirty minutes to accomplish what his right hand had done in twenty. But he'd done it! Yeah!

More applause, with the addition of a high-five, accompanied by another broad grin from the lady with the buff arms, and Wes felt odd, admitting Mary's approval was almost as good as her kisses.

He gestured for her to sit again, and she eased onto his lap, looking a little wary. "How much 'hands' are you planning to use?"

"You'll have to kiss me to find out."

Raising a brow but taking his dare, she tilted her head the opposite way from the last kiss and started a slow, seductive kiss that had his hands wandering around her back and down her arms in record time. She nibbled his lower lip and a low growl escaped his throat. His hands shot down to her hips and grabbed hold, kneading her firm skin and pulling her closer. He wanted her. All of her.

Shocked by the revelation, he was the one to break the kiss. Wouldn't taking this any further just be frustrating for both of them?

"That was nice," she said, dreamy-eyed.

He bit back his first thought—*That's about as far as we can go. Ever.* Logically, he knew it wasn't so, but he didn't have a shred of proof from his own body. Still, making out with Mary was a hell of a great way to pass the day. "I thought we were just getting started."

"Sorry to break it to you, but we've got more work to do." She got off his lap again, but not before he could see the tightened tips of her breasts through her clingy workout top. So he hadn't lost his touch.

He'd woken up grumpy and frustrated, as he did many mornings, and had planned to work it off with dumbbells, but now he'd accomplished some death-defying acts of sleight of hand, and been paid in kisses and a quick feel up of his rehab coach. What else would this day bring? So he grinned, and as far as he was concerned, if Mary kept kissing him, they could sit there all afternoon rolling coins through fingers.

But now what was that mischievous twinkle in her eye about? The day just kept getting better and better, and he didn't have to wait long to find out.

In the next second she produced another small

box from her shoulder bag, and he was sure the thing had a trapdoor inside.

"And what's this?" Admittedly, he began to feel excited, like a kid on Christmas morning with a special trapdoor stocking. Especially if he kept bargaining for kisses.

"Chinese exercise balls. They're meant to improve finger dexterity."

He spurted a laugh at the explanation, the first he'd laughed in days. What would she think of next? As the old saying went, *If my friends could see me now.*

She opened the box and showed him how to hold the two balls in the palm of his hand and rotate them over and over. "The goal is for the balls not to touch. Eventually. It takes a lot of practice, but we've got time."

He dutifully took the balls, getting a feel for them. "And you just happened to have these lying around?"

"I go to PT conferences for continuing education. You'd be surprised what the vendors give out."

From first-hand experience, he knew about

medical conferences and product vendors, and bought her story without question about how she'd acquired the Chinese balls. He worked them in his palm first with one hand then the other, liking the slick metallic feel of them. They seemed cold and slippery and he had to be careful not to let one drop. He also realized his hands were getting tired from all of the dexterity tests that morning, which meant she'd been right—he was out of shape in the hand department.

"Work on those this afternoon and tonight. Both hands."

"Yes, ma'am."

"Tomorrow we're going to thread tiny beads."

"Why do I suddenly feel like I'm ten again and back in summer camp?"

"It's just part of the process, Wes." She smiled, and it lit up the room again.

An ordinary expression shouldn't be that noticeable, but coming from her—plump lips parted over naturally spaced teeth, lips he'd tasted and liked, the smile easily infecting her eyes—it was extraordinary. Everything she did for him seemed larger than life, yet humble and sweet, and always forced him to get too close to her, her kisses the prize he wanted to keep winning.

"Well, if neurosurgery isn't in my future, maybe I can get a job as a sleight of hand magician somewhere?"

And there was that beam again, as if it was a beacon showing him the way to happiness, touching his heart and a whole lot of other places. He juggled the metal balls in his palm faster and faster, looking forward to the rest of the day, and especially their dinner that night. Alone. With Rita banished once she'd set everything up for the meal.

For a guy who'd woken up grumpy, things were definitely looking up.

For the first time since his accident he believed he might be able to pick up the skills he'd once honed, and continue with his professional life again. Before now, he'd refused to consider it, especially after attempting to return to the hospital too soon, and experiencing full throttle failure. Not to mention humiliation. No longer able to juggle patients with ease and conviction, he'd fumbled with simple things like holding a laptop on his lap and wheeling himself into an examination room. He'd had to face colleagues feeling less than their equal. When he'd bumped into an examination table and set off leg spasms, he'd had enough. His ears heated with the memories. After a few days of denying the truth, he'd had to admit defeat and return home feeling lost.

Never a quitter, that's when he'd gone even more manic in the gym, and for his efforts he'd never felt physically stronger in his life. From the waist up. Yet he was still so insecure about returning to his life's vocation. The job he'd felt called to do since he was a teenager.

Now, here he was with news about a special stand-up wheelchair, and Mary with a deck of cards, a quarter, some odd little balls, plus a promise to string beads tomorrow. The crazy thing was, every little part of the day's equation had made him feel anything was possible again. Looking at life through new eyes, he felt ready to say, *Why not?*

He watched her across the room, setting up for

their passive range of motion session, and took a moment to marvel over how she'd opened up his world to the possible again. It wasn't sleight of hand magic she peddled either. She spoke the truth. Honest and practical. And for that he'd always be grateful.

Like a spear to the chest, it hit him. She'd signed on for two months, and one had already passed. He'd miss her when she left. A sensation he'd compartmentalized for months forced its way out—giving a damn. He cared about her, looked forward to seeing her every day, and would definitely miss her when she packed up that tiny house and moved on.

With her help he'd go back to work and become part of the living again, even though he wasn't at all sure he was ready to join that group.

Mary showed up on time for dinner, worrying about her choice of clothes—her best black slacks and a clingy blue patterned top that might show a little too much cleavage. After their kissing game earlier, she didn't know what to expect from Wes.

One thing she did know for sure, though, she liked it!

She'd called out once she'd gotten to his front door.

"It's open. I'm in the kitchen."

She didn't want Wes to think she was trying to seduce him with her choice of clothes, but she wanted to look nice, and this top came with a definite dip of cleavage. From the appreciative gaze in Wesley's eyes when she walked into his kitchen, she figured she'd made a good choice.

"Wow, something smells delicious!"

"I owe my amazing cooking skills to Rita, who had the good sense to prepare all the ingredients for our meal and take off, leaving me with the easy cooking part."

Hadn't he said he used Rita when he wanted to impress his date? Was she considered a date or an old friend? And did old friends find multiple excuses to kiss each other? Man, she was confused.

"Must be nice." She could only imagine what it would be like to have a personal sous chef. She'd never been in his kitchen and was blown over by the huge marble-topped island, all the high-end appliances and a breakfast nook large enough to throw a party in. Heck, it was the size of her entire kitchen! This for a guy who lived like a recluse.

He led her to the dining room, just around the corner from that breakfast room. He had a casserole dish on his lap as he rolled the wheelchair, and she worried it might be burning his legs and he didn't know it. "May I take that for you?"

"I've got it."

Dumb question. She needed to learn to let him be independent without rushing to his aid. If her hope was for him to feel whole again, she shouldn't interfere with his process. *Let him be a man.*

The dining table nearly took her breath away. He'd chosen a cozy area with a splendid view of the ocean, with light naturally stained table and chairs, making her think of beach chic, whatever that was. The dishes were brightly patterned and she picked one up to see where it had been made.

"Got those on a trip to Spain."

Oh, the life he must have led BP. Before paraplegia. "They're beautiful." The yellow patterned dishes with dark blue highlights picked up the midnight blue drapes bracketing the long line of windows.

"Come, help me bring out the rest of the food. All that sleight of hand stuff makes a guy hungry."

After a couple more trips back and forth to the kitchen, their table was set, but before he took his place at the head, where she'd noticed no chair had been placed, he opened a drawer in the sideboard. Soon he rolled from candle to candle placed all along the buffet and at several stations across the expansive table, as he used the candle lighter. Once done, he turned off the overhead lights and gestured for her to sit next to him, but not before he fiddled with something on the wall, next to the electric switch. *Voilà!* Music. Soft, strings and piano. Perfect.

With chills across her shoulders she sat, watching the man she'd seen every day in the gym for the last few days, and who she'd recently started kissing for pure pleasure. He was on his own turf and he looked nothing short of handsome and confident, and for that she let fly a quick, secret dream. *What if?*

He opened a bottle of red wine and poured each of them a glass, then removed the lid from their appetizer dish.

"Wow, that looks great."

"Good, you like shrimp. This is my version of shrimp cocktail. I sauté them and serve them warm. Help yourself." He handed her the platter and she dug right in.

"You made this?"

"Spent the last hour and a half getting everything ready for us."

"What about Rita?"

"She bought everything I'd need and had all the ingredients right where I wanted them."

"That's great. So you like cooking?"

"Sometimes. If there's a lady I want to impress."

She stopped, shrimp midway to her mouth. Their eyes met and she saw the flash of interest. She'd felt it earlier when they'd kissed too. The chills returned and she knew tonight was going to be different. "Well, thank you, then. I'm definitely impressed."

Over spinach salad with pancetta and feta cheese Wes seemed to relax. "I used to do all the cooking when I was with Giselle."

"Your ex-fiancée?"

He nodded and took another bite.

She wondered why he'd brought Giselle up, especially since they'd been seeming to slip into something more serious the more time they spent around each other. She worried she was setting herself up for a fall by thinking a few kisses meant something to Wes. According to Alex, he'd never been without lady friends.

"I forget, was she fiancée one or fiancée two?"

He ignored her dig, but went serious. "My fiancées never stood a chance, I suppose, not with how work was my total world and all. Emma found someone else to make her happy and Giselle married her job, just like I did." He'd jumped off on a subject that nearly made her drop her fork.

"Are you saying you think it was your fault?"

He served New York steak strips with smashed

potatoes, and the heavier food seemed compatible with the topic of conversation. "I feel like I squandered any chance of being in a solid relationship, you know, that *one* you mentioned the first day we worked out, that 'special one'. I never believed in it before and now it's too late."

"Why do you say that? You're talking like your life is over, and that's just not true." Why couldn't she get through to him?

"It would be really tough to get involved with a guy like me. I'm a special needs guy now."

"You're the same person inside you've always been. That's the part that attracts people."

After two failed engagements, Wes was hell bent on never opening his heart again, had his excuses lined up and waiting, and she didn't have time for him to figure things out. Besides, she'd already been through that with her one and only fiancé, Chuck. From him she'd learned if a guy didn't want you, he simply didn't want you, and there was nothing she could do to change that. Yet, foolishly, she had tried.

Like Wes focusing on his job back when he'd been engaged, these days all she wanted to focus on was becoming a mother. Holding a baby of her own in her arms, loving and protecting it was her number one goal, and she couldn't let anything stand in the way. Especially not a guy unwilling to accept there was life after paraplegia.

"I'll give you this, Harris," he said, forking a piece of steak and mixing it with potatoes before eating it.

She waited as he chewed, taking a dainty bite in case she needed to prod him along.

"You've brought life back into this house. It had gotten dreary and lonely, but now things have changed. That's all thanks to you, and don't choke on your steak but that means a lot to me."

He'd been refilling his glass with dark red wine, and she was sure he'd never broach this topic if it wasn't for the magic of vino. She was so grateful he had, because he'd just paid her an amazing compliment.

"And that means a lot to me, too, Wes. I came here because I'm an old family friend and I wanted to help."

"And my sister begged you to come."

"And *I am* a family friend, did I mention that?"

He winked at her, and damn if that didn't give her a quick thrill. She almost forgot what she was going to say. Oh, right. "So we got off to a rocky start, but I'm super happy with where you're at now."

"Cheers." He raised his glass and smiled, his eyes showing the effect of the couple of glasses he'd enjoyed, as he charmingly ignored what she'd just said.

She drank more and admitted he'd chosen the perfect wine to complement the steak and potatoes. The wine warmed her insides, and also loosened her lips. He was opening up, why shouldn't she? So she decided to be supportive of his reaching out by giving her a huge compliment. Coming from him, that was a big deal. "Just so you know, I can totally understand how you feel about it being too late. I've given up on finding the right life partner, too. But here's the crazy part. I've always prided myself on being a free spirit, you know, independent and self-reliant. Heck, I never had anyone to depend on until I met your family." She took another sip of wine, choosing to hold the glass nearby rather than put it down.

"But guess what, since meeting your youngest niece, Rose, this free spirit wants more than anything to have a baby."

There, she'd finally admitted it to someone, and it didn't sound so crazy, did it? She took another sip of wine just in case it did seem like a whacky idea, and watched the expression change on his face.

Wes stared at her for a few seconds, digesting what she'd confessed, looking so serious she chose to think he was treating her secret with great care, and she deeply appreciated that. So she drank more wine to give him time to mull things over.

Before she realized it, he rolled his wheelchair over to her and took both of her hands in his. "So is this our secret?"

She nodded.

"Crazy, isn't it? Neither of us ever expects to find 'the one'. I don't have a clue if I can have sex, and you want to be a mother. Does that sum things up?"

Put that way, she had to laugh. "I know. Crazy, right?" But it felt good to finally tell someone.

"It's not crazy, Mary, if that's what you want. You'd be a great mom, too." He pulled her close and kissed her gently, then reached around her shoulders and hugged her.

The hug felt like home, so she kissed him back. He hesitated briefly but soon his lips complied and a simple kiss suddenly turned into much more. Then it ended far too fast.

He stared seriously at her. "So it seems we both have something to prove. Me going back to work and you putting your uterus to work."

"Something like that." She grinned and was grateful he hadn't laughed her out of his house, though her thoughts were still hung up on the far-too-brief make-out session from the moment before.

He stared at her for a long moment, and she projected that he was thinking the same thing she was about the ramifications of his last statement. He wanted to have sex again and she wanted to have a baby. They both had something to prove and she was helping him so maybe he should help her? Or maybe she was reading far too much into his sympathetic expression.

He backed his chair away. “Are you ready for dessert?”

“There’s more?”

“How about some grilled peaches with ricotta and honey?”

“Yes, please.”

“Great. So come into the kitchen and let’s get cooking.”

“I’m making dessert?”

“No. You’re watching me make dessert. I just want your company.”

They’d both drunk enough wine to open up on topics they’d kept close to their chests until to-night. They definitely didn’t need to drink any-more. “How about I make some coffee?”

Wesley worked diligently grilling peaches then spreading them with the sugar and cinna-mon mixture as he thought what a total disas-ter it would be to try to make love to Mary. It would be a total clinical trial and humiliating, so humiliating, and it was the last thing he’d ever want to face. Yet, putting his pride and wheel-chair aside, the thought of being with Mary made his head spin. What he’d give to go back in time and take her the way he wanted to now. He'd had the chance, was sure of that, back then. Now she needed someone to help her get pregnant, not someone who didn't even know if he could still function in that department.

In a far less festive mood now, he served dessert with the coffee she'd made, and they ate in silence. The sweet-tasting peach hardly registered with his brain, because he couldn't get the thought of helping her get pregnant out of his mind. After all she'd done for him, why shouldn't he volunteer? Maybe he couldn't take her to bed like he'd prefer, but he sure as hell could still be a sperm donor. The ramifications of fathering a baby he'd never be involved with didn't sound appealing. He'd never really thought about being a dad, but he sure as hell knew if he ever became one, he'd want to act like one. Not some donor with no say.

"We've got an early start tomorrow," she said, out of the blue. Probably because he'd gone missing with his thoughts. "I'd better get home."

Damn, he'd really blown the mood he'd so carefully set earlier. He'd wanted tonight to be special, he'd even started to open up to her about his failed engagements, then he'd let insecurity hold him back. Now she'd taken the "all business" route. "Ah, yes, tomorrow we make jewelry from tiny beads."

"Yup. Can I help with the dishes first?"

"Nope. That's the beauty of Rita. She'll take care of everything in the morning."

"So that's how the other half lives. Must be nice." She strolled and he rolled toward the front door.

"Hey, don't knock my life of privilege until you've tried it." He knew she'd grown up the hard way, but never felt she'd held a grudge toward him about it. Now that he spent his days in a wheelchair, he figured the playing field was level. Who could envy him?

"Tomorrow we'll work on strengthening your abs, to get you ready for that standing wheelchair I see in your future."

She never gave up, and that endeared her to him all the more. "Yes, boss. It sounds nuts, but I can almost see myself performing surgery again."

"You will, Wes. I know it."

He tugged on her hand and brought her closer. "And I see a baby in your future."

"Do you?"

The excitement on her face nearly broke his heart. He promised something he had no business getting mixed up in, but it didn't stop him. "I'm sure of it."

"Thank you."

"I'm going to tell you something, but don't let it go to your head, Harris. I like having you around."

She gave a flirty gaze. "Then don't let this go to your head either. I like being around."

He brought her face down to his and kissed her, because he couldn't stand another second without touching and tasting her. Wishing he had that standing wheelchair right now, he'd give anything to be on her level. Eye to eye. Mouth to mouth. Her breasts mashed against his chest and his hands wandering anywhere they liked.

But kissing her from this angle wasn't half-bad. In fact, right now, since she sat on his lap, he couldn't think of any place he'd rather be, as long as they were sharing a kiss.

Where were they going with all these kisses, anyway? What did it mean that they couldn't seem to keep their lips apart? Was it a promise of good things to come? The thought of getting his hopes up sent a shudder through him. Or maybe it was the sensation of her tongue slipping over his that set that off.

He'd gone off at the deep end, imagining all kinds of miracles happening between them, and drinking three glasses of wine had to be the reason.

Yeah, that had to be it. The wine. Because there was no way he'd let a sexy, exciting and wonderful woman like Mary Harris get hooked up with him.

She deserved far more than a guy stuck in a chair.

CHAPTER SIX

TWO DAYS LATER, Mary and Wesley worked side by side on the high parallel bars. He used the strength of his arms to move forward, and had just made it along the bar.

"Can you turn and go back?" Mary asked, dropping off the bars to watch. "I'll spot you."

Obviously unsure of this bright idea of hers, he passed her a warning look. "Like hell you will. If I let go and fall, I'll be dead weight and bring you down with me."

"You won't let go."

"And you know this how?"

"I know you, Wes. You've got this. You're the strongest guy I know." *And the best looking and the smartest and the sexiest.* Her encouragement must have given him the last bit of confidence he needed because he pressed upward in stiff arm gymnastics style, swung and switched hands to face in the opposite direction, then walked his hands back to the other side. When he got to the end he dropped to his armpits on the bars and let out a yelp.

"What's wrong?"

"Cramp. Got a cramp."

She rushed to his aid, and with her helping him balanced against her she eased him to the mat. He grimaced and grabbed his shoulder near his neck. She massaged the area, feeling the golf-ball-sized knot. It didn't let up.

"Lie down. Wait right here." She rushed to the pile of gym towels, ran one under water in the kitchenette in the corner of the gym, wrung it out and popped it into the microwave for a quick heat up. Once done she whirled it round and round to cool it off a bit, then placed it on Wesley's shoulders. "Still tight?"

He clenched his teeth and continued to rub the area. "Yes."

At the top of his head, she leaned over him and again massaged his neck and shoulder muscles with a deep and intentional touch, finding the unchanged knot, as tight as before. He groaned, but in a good way, so she continued until she felt the muscle on the right side loosen and finally let go. But she didn't stop. She made fists and rolled her knuckles round and round on his trapezius muscles to keep the spasm from returning, then switched back to the deep massage. Finally, she slid her flattened hands beneath his upper back and pushed in and out, locating a nerve bundle on each side below his scapula and pressing her fingers upward. He moaned, sounding in ecstasy. She pressed and released several times until she felt him relax completely.

"I let you down, Harris."

"No, you didn't."

"When I was up there, I pretended my legs still worked, and I got a little cocky trying to swing myself like a real gymnast. That dead weight put a quick stop to that fantasy." He rubbed his forehead. "Never realized how strong those gymnast guys are."

"Could have fooled me. You were the master of those bars from where I stood."

He made a pained laugh. “Yeah. I won all right.”

She sat back on her heels, let her hands slip from his shoulders.

“Don’t stop,” he whispered, then reached up and grasped a wrist, pulling her forward until her face was above his. She continued to gently massage both shoulders for several more silent moments.

“Come and lie down with me.”

The invitation was too deliciously inviting to resist. She scooted beside him and curled toward his torso, and now that his cramp was gone he wrapped his arm around her, pulling her close. Oh, how wonderful it felt to be skin to skin, finally getting to explore all of his hard work with the touch of her fingertips. “You looked incredibly sexy up there.”

“Yeah? How do you like me now?”

They laughed gently together and seeing him devoid of his usual defenses—vulnerable and open—turned out to be the most powerful aphrodisiac she’d ever experienced. Off and on she’d gotten peeks at this part of the formerly borderline arrogant and commanding man, and she definitely liked this side of his personality best.

A wicked thought popped into her mind. What she'd give to straddle him, then watch him contort from the feel of her, this time in a pleasurable way, not in pain.

Her thoughts worked like a bellows on the fire that always seemed to simmer between them. Surely he felt it too? She rose up and planted a full-on kiss on his welcoming mouth. He pulled her down on top of him, she stretched like a cat and deepened the kiss, showing him what she wished they could do with their bodies.

"This is highly unprofessional," she said over his lips after a particularly mind-boggling make-out session.

"You don't work for me," he said quickly, pulling her mouth back on target.

After that she stopped thinking and went with the feeling whirling inside her, heating her, making her super sensitive to his every touch. Minutes and more minutes slipped by as they kissed and she squirmed over him. He scouted her tightened breasts with his fingertips, soon taking them into his hands. She fought the urge to throw off her gym top, but something held her back. She really shouldn't be doing this, yet she could kiss him all day. She grew damp between her legs, and he must have sensed they were nearing a point of no return.

He broke off the heated kiss, the fire in his darkened eyes turning to anger. "What's the point of getting all worked up when I can't—?"

Damn, she'd crossed the line with him. "What we were doing felt great. What's wrong with that?"

He thinned his lips, shutting down right before her eyes. "I've worked enough today. Shoulder's still acting up. I'm ready for a break."

The snub stung deep, making all the wonderful sensations she'd just enjoyed disappear. "Okay." She rolled off him, grateful she hadn't shed her top when she'd wanted to, thinking how exposed she would have felt sitting half-naked in front of him. He didn't want her. That was clear. "Let me help you into your chair."

"I can do it myself." He sounded defensive, or tired of her not getting the point he was independent. He didn't need her help. Every barrier they'd broken down quickly got put back in place.

She rolled his chair to him so he could do his thing and put himself in it from the floor. The stunt always amazed her, especially how easy he made it look. "So that's it for today, then?"

"Yeah." He didn't make eye contact. "See you tomorrow."

And he left.

At a loss for what to say or do, and especially how to feel, she stood there and watched him roll away. She needed to get out of that gym where just moments ago she had nearly been in heaven, kissing and loving the man she wanted with all her might to help. The man who'd have nothing to do with her beyond his comfort zone. He liked to call her the dominatrix, but he was the one in complete control. Over the past couple of weeks they'd ventured into showing their affection for each other with kisses. Each session got more daring than the next. Today they'd taken a huge leap forward—she'd straddled him!—and now several steps back. She'd pushed her desire too far. He obviously wasn't ready for the next step.

Her stomach twisted and her hands fisted and opened several times while she stared at the closed door. She needed to get out of here now. It was time to pay the beach a visit. Maybe fighting with waves would help get her mind off Wesley, the guy who turned her on but wanted nothing to do with her.

What a mess.

Wes had showered and now dried himself, remembering the feel of Mary's hands on his shoulders, massaging him, easing his tension. Then she'd taken his mouth and driven him mad with her insistence. He'd fought every thought, and the desire to have her, but had given in. She'd felt incredible, and her breasts had nearly done him in. She'd made him forget how he'd changed, and all he'd felt had been desire. With everything he had, he'd wanted to take her, to be inside her. Then he'd remembered who he was now, how he had no idea how to take a woman, and their sexy moment had vaporized.

Any woman would get tired of that unfulfilled promise soon enough. She'd deny it until the day she died, too, because that was the way Mary Harris was. No way would he tie her—or her free spirit—down.

From the bathroom window he glanced out at the ocean. There she was, jogging toward the waves in a tiny bikini, her slender, toned legs displaying the muscles from all her hard work. With nothing but a towel across his lap, he rolled into his bedroom for a better view. She dove into the water, swimming past the first few waves, then, like the female warrior she was, fiercely swam to catch the next, successfully catching and riding it nearly to the sand.

Had she been as tied up in knots as he'd been when they'd wrapped their bodies together? He watched her stand up on the beach, turn and watch the waves, kick some sand, then head back in. He couldn't help but notice how her swimsuit had tucked itself into her high and tight rear end. His hands had felt that fine curve the day they'd played their racy little game of quarter roll. Damn, she looked sexy. An odd flickering feeling circled low in his abdomen.

Enjoying the distant sensation somewhere

below his belly—his groin?—he watched her swim out and take another wave, body surfing, getting lifted and dumped onto the sand. She laughed, standing covered in caked-on sand, wiping some away from her chest, skimming the tops of her breasts above that string called a top. The breasts he'd finally felt and longed to taste earlier. Unfazed by getting beat up by the water, she swam out again. It made him smile. After a few false starts she caught another swell that lifted her and carried her as she perfected her swimming strokes, all the way to shore until she stood and walked the rest of the way in. That was the woman he'd known since she was a teenager, she never gave up. Obviously satisfied with her accomplishment, she rolled out her towel and plopped on top.

Damn if he didn't want her more than anything he'd ever wanted in his life. Beneath the towel he felt himself, surprised by what he found—a full erection.

He'd never admitted to anyone the real reason he'd broken his engagement with Giselle. Aside from her having a sexy name, she wasn't the woman he'd hoped she'd be in bed. Once a week had never been enough for his voracious appetite, yet their schedules had dictated every facet of their lives. She'd seemed satisfied. He hadn't been in the least.

He'd gone to his sister's wedding and had had his overpriced socks knocked off, making out with Mary. Half-tipsy or not, they'd known what they were doing, and she'd turned him on like Giselle never had. How could he marry her after that?

Taking one last glance at Mary on her beach towel, Wes longed to be there beside her.

He rolled into his bedroom and opened his laptop, typing into the browser and searching. A list of websites came up. One in particular held his interest, and within minutes he placed an order for some things that would accommodate positions for sex and also enhance natural movements during intercourse for a paraplegic. A gliding chair and an extra bouncy cot. Who knew two such practical-looking items could turn a guy on? But they did. He was on fire. Not that he needed any help at the moment, with Mary's bikini-clad image burning behind his eyes.

Still revved up, he explored the plethora of information out there on the web about paraplegics and sex, and spent the rest of the afternoon engrossed and admittedly titillated by the provocative reading.

The next morning, Mary wasn't sure what she'd find when she showed up at Wes's gym. Drawing on extra courage, she popped her head out the door to the hallway. "Wes! Are you there?" Nothing.

She ventured down the hall toward his room. "Wes?" It was a long hallway, huge like the rest of the house, so she kept walking, worry creeping its way under her skin. What if he'd gotten sick last night, or had injured himself? Surely he had emergency pull cords in strategic areas? Or maybe he'd just had it with her? Her nerves twisted at the thought.

"Wes?" Though her pace slowed, she continued cautiously onward, worry working its way through every cell. She thought she heard conversation coming from his room, so she stopped and listened harder. Not conversation. The television. She stepped up and knocked on his bedroom door. “Wes? Are you in there?”

“I’m busy,” he called out.

“You’re not sick or injured?”

“No.”

The conversation on the television seemed to have stopped. She listened harder. Heavy breathing and moans had taken its place. *What the hell?* Was someone in there with him?

Antonio! Antonio! Oh, ah, ah, ah.

Okay, wait minute. What was going on in there? A big fat wave of adrenaline coupled with jealousy washed over her as she knocked and pushed her way through the door. She had no clue what she’d find, but she needed to see.

Obvious sounds of a couple going at it emitted from the laptop he watched from his bed. He wasn’t sick or injured, there was that, so her nerves settled the tiniest bit. But he hadn’t gotten out of bed yet, and he was obviously watching… “Porn? You’re watching porn at this hour?”

His eyes never left the screen. "Didn't realize there was a designated viewing time."

"You know what I mean."

"Look at this. Come look at the size of…"

"What are you doing, Wes?"

Finally, he broke away from the computer and cast her a defiant gaze. "You mean, what am I not doing, as in not going to work out."

"Why not?"

"I'm taking the day off. Even you said I should do that once in a while." The woman's squeals of ecstasy made it impossible to follow his conversation. "Join me?"

He'd staged quite a dramatic way to tell her he'd had enough of their "friendship-workout partnership", especially after yesterday when she'd tried to seduce him. Could she blame him? She certainly had some making up to do.

Against her better judgment, she took the last few steps toward his bed. "Holy Long John Silver, Batman, that *is* big!"

He slanted a sideways glance her way, the corner of his mouth twitching just the tiniest bit. Good, she'd gotten through to him. She wasn't the enemy. She really was here to help him step back into the life he'd left behind. Why couldn't she get that through his head?

Seriously, the guy was one thing, but how did a woman ever lie on her stomach with an enhanced chest like that?

"You did tell me I could still have sex."

"No one can have sex like that! That's impossible. Geez, I think that position has been computer generated or enhanced, or whatever it is they do these days."

He laughed outright. "I used to do that all the time."

It was her turn to laugh as she shifted toward him with a huge questioning gaze, and thank God it lightened the tense, for oh-so-many reasons moment. "You did?" She tried to mix deadpan with a hint of interest.

He cracked a genuine smile. "Maybe not exactly like that." Yay, she'd won! What, exactly, she didn't know, but he didn't feel nearly as belligerent as when she'd first walked in. Progress. "I'm just saying you did promise me."

"Absolutely, but within reason."

"Oh, so now you're backtracking."

"No. No, I'm not. You *can* have sex."

With those piercing coffee-tinted eyes he stared at her then shut down and closed the computer, all the while watching her. Once the soundtrack had gone quiet he reached for her wrist, lightly grasping her flesh. "Show me."

Do not chicken out now. It was the second time he'd asked her to prove to him he could have sex. Gratifying sex. His dare had everything to do with a plea for help, and it was her one opportunity to help him cross that huge barrier keeping him from feeling part of the living. Or, more specifically, a complete man. Getting back to work would only solve half of the problem. This, the most personal of all issues, could possibly be more intimidating than performing neurosurgery again. She needed to tread lightly, and make sure she got right her one shot at proving him wrong.

She needed to buy herself time to gather her thoughts. "I don't intend to prove a damn thing with you lying in bed in your pajamas. Once you've showered and dressed, meet me in the gym." And off she trotted as though she knew exactly how to handle this most unusual request.

At the door, she turned to find Wes was the one with a dumbfounded gaze. Good. It gave her an idea. "While you're getting ready, I want you to think about one important thing. Don't ever forget the brain is by far the biggest sex organ." She walked out the door. "Even bigger than those things on that woman's chest."

She hoped she'd left him smiling instead of scowling.

Twenty minutes later, Wes rolled into the gym where she'd done some quick research on top of her searches in the past and set up her own laptop.

He looked determined, with his computer on his lap. Good, he was here to do some serious work on a very serious issue. It gave her courage to bring up the new techniques she'd learned about from talking to her former patient, Sean, the other day. Fortunately Sean was a guy who had zero inhibitions about his personal life. After their long conversation, she felt well schooled on the subject of paraplegic sex.

"I'm ready if you are," he said.

"You certainly look better." And once he was closer she kept her next thought to herself—*You smell great, too.*

He smiled easily, and reached out to touch her hip, an intimate gesture that helped her realize they were both adults and she liked it when he touched her as much as she hoped he liked her to do so. Her free arm dropped around his shoulders. Hey, if they were about to get down and dirty, theoretically speaking, they may as well be comfortable with each other.

He opened his laptop and clicked, then turned it her way. "Read this."

She opened the blog titled "Confessions of a Paraplegic's Girlfriend", and found the author had written in detail about the various ways she and her boyfriend pleased each other. She read silently, with obvious interest, how oral sex for both partners was a great start, how her partner was able to have an erection watching her give him oral sex, and how she was able to keep him firm with her hand and then mount him and bring herself to orgasm. How her pleasure turned her boyfriend on to the point of experiencing fluttering in his lower abdomen as she orgasmed and he swore he could feel her tightening around him, and how eventually her undivided attention to him brought about ejaculation.

Mary swallowed quietly, turned on, her mouth having grown dry reading the exquisitely intimate and thorough descriptions.

She'd call the writing erotic since reading the blog had aroused her, and she assumed it had done the same for Wes.

"I told you," she said, finding it difficult to meet his eyes, and immediately flitting away when she did. Only then did she realize her nipples had hardened and he'd noticed through the thin fabric of her bra and white top.

He took his time lifting his gaze from her chest to meet her eyes. "You did. But I found this. And more."

"You've definitely got my attention." Suddenly feeling winded, she inhaled.

"Good," he said, latching on to her stare, which arced between them and with it traveled sexy vibrations that dove and zinged throughout her upper body.

He subtly lifted his brows and toggled to another website. “This one is less erotic but very practical.”

She clicked on what looked like a small canvas cot divided into two parts—an open-sided, low sitting chair, which glided, and a cot which was far less cumbersome than a bed, and allowed a paraplegic’s partner easier maneuverability and access, with built-in natural bounce.

“It’s called the glide rider with extra bounce,” he said, serious as hell.

Mary pulled in her chin, needing to take another deep breath while he explained how the contraption might work and the number of positions it could allow.

Her face went hot. She was definitely turned on, but for the sake of science she went along with him as he explained step by step the sexual process using the gliding chair. Their heads were nearly touching as they both studied the computer screen, Wes using the mouse cursor like a laser light on the various parts of the contraptions. His lime and spice aftershave invaded her nose, and she hoped her tropical garden shampoo excited him half as much as she tried to concentrate on the website.

He'd certainly been doing his research.

He lifted her hair and kissed her neck, surprising her. She sat straighter, acutely aware of his lips tripping down her neck, igniting the length of her spine. She inhaled then held her breath to fight off a flood of shivers. Unsuccessfully.

"This is turning me on, you know that, right?" he said in a low husky voice.

His whiskey-tinged voice was turning her on, too, not to mention those feathery kisses on her neck. "I thought it was the other way around," she said, trying not to sound breathy.

"Something's obviously working." He glanced at his lap, where his arousal was in full form beneath his jeans.

Surprised and happy, she smiled softly at him. "I told you."

He continued playing with her hair. "Normally I hate it when you say that, but I'll forgive you this time."

"Gee, thanks."

He nuzzled her neck, sending more tingles across her skin, and she involuntarily clenched her inner thigh muscles.

"So how do we order it?"

"I already have." The man was definitely taking the lead on a new version of his sex life.

She let her grin stretch from one side of her face to the other, like a kid unable to keep a secret. "A two-day delivery?"

"Sorry we have to wait that long, but yes."

We? Seeing the hunger in his eyes, feeling it herself, knowing his need to prove he was still a complete man, she quickly sorted through their situation. She was his friend, but they'd moved way beyond that now. In his own way, he'd been courting her, and he definitely wanted her. If she was honest, she'd admit how much she wanted him, too.

How would they make things work? She traveled. Would leave in a few weeks for another state to be determined. He planned to stay put. To resume his medical career. But this one thing, this pure desire arcing between them right now, was the one exact thing—if it worked out the way she hoped—that could unite them for life. Even if they never saw each other again.

He needed her to help him prove he was still a man.

And she needed him for an equally touchy task.

A baby.

Nothing ventured, nothing gained. Why not go for it?

She swallowed away the dryness in her throat in order to speak. "You're the smartest and best-looking man I've ever known. You want to have sex." Her voice started to tremble. "And I want a baby."

From his wide open stare, just short of going slack-jawed, she knew she had his attention so she plunged ahead.

"Will you consider making a bargain with me?"

CHAPTER SEVEN

MARY'S OFFER OF striking a bargain sent all the sexy feelings flying. His need to hold her in his arms? Gone. His erection? Also gone. He'd never given a thought to becoming a father. Not without a wife, and with two unsuccessful engagements he'd yet to find the right woman. Once he'd become a paraplegic, to be honest, he'd never given parenting another thought.

A business deal. Was that what she'd just suggested?

Wes sat staring at Mary, considering how far they'd come and how so suddenly off track they'd gotten. He needed to clarify. "A bargain as in signing a contract? 'Must have X number of sexual encounters and produce one offspring. Or all prior encounters will be null and void'?"

With an earnest expression, taking his hands

into hers, she said, "You know that's not what I'm talking about. There could never be anything so cold and hard between us." She glanced at his lap, where he hadn't disappeared nearly as much as he'd thought. "Well, cold anyway. Wes, come on, we have an opportunity to each provide something life-changing for the other. It's a proposition only people who trust each other can make, and I trust you. Will you think about it?"

The tips of her ears had gone red and he understood how difficult this must be for her to bring up. As tough, if not more, than it had been for him when he'd asked her to have sex with him—just so he could prove he could. Why hadn't he thought about the procreation part? She'd been straightforward about wanting a child before since she'd hit some magical age, and he'd understood how she might want that, but right here and now? With him doing the honors? She asked far too much. He couldn't just impregnate and go. If he had a kid he'd want to be a part of their life.

"I've definitely got to think this through." He sent her a warning glance for changing the serious topic of having sex into an even more serious subject of making a baby.

"I understand, but if you agree, please know I'd never hold you accountable for my child."

"What kind of man do you think I am? Of course I'd want to be involved." He scrubbed his face in frustration. "Look, we're not even sure this pregnancy can be produced, but you know as well as I do how surprises pop into life all the time. Like me having an accident. Something could happen to you. I wouldn't want a kid staring me in the eyes, asking why he or she never knew I was their dad."

"I know I've taken you by surprise."

"Far beyond that, Harris. Bargaining for a baby?" Though initially appalled by her request, Wesley couldn't hide the part of him that found the deal sexy as hell. It must have shown in his eyes because she gave a demure smile—one that attempted to hide the obvious adult-woman-bargaining-sex-for-personal-reward-who-has-just-blown-potential-partner's-mind. The sweet expression didn't come close to covering the truth—she'd sleep with him—and damn if he didn't find that sexy. As hell.

"I'm not trying to trap you into anything, Wes, and I'll sign any document you want to prove it."

Was he ready or willing for the rest of her bargain? He needed to give becoming a father at this stage in his life some serious consideration.

Playing the "cool" card, he rolled his chair backward. *Yeah, he did stuff like this all the time, bargained for sex. Further proof how worldly he used to be. Not!*

"I'm going to think about this today, and I'll be in touch." Off he went to his office in hopes of wrapping his mind around what she'd just suggested, and trying really hard to keep his mind from imagining the possibilities. In front of her, anyway.

Having sex again would be great, but the thing that struck him the hardest was the possibility of becoming a dad. A crazy sense of hope frightened him. He'd let go of so many dreams after his accident, but here was Mary pushing her way back into his life, forcing him to feel alive again, filled with desire, and now daring him to consider making a baby. Was he ready for that?

After thirty-seven years, one thing he knew about himself—once he put his mind to something, nothing could stop him.

Mary's cellphone rang around two in the afternoon while she sunbathed on the beach. It was Wes. Immediately her pulse tripled. "Hi. Worked things out yet?"

She held her breath in anticipation of his answer, praying he wouldn't say no. But also scared to death he'd say yes, because it would change everything between them, and she'd really gotten to like being Wes Van Allen's friend.

"Have dinner with me tonight." It wasn't a question but a statement, and suddenly she could breathe again. "We'll go to Geoffrey's. I'll pick you up at seven." After a pause when she expected him to hang up, because a guy in control of her future didn't need an answer knowing how much this meant to her, he said, "Oh, and wear something sexy."

She couldn't be sure what he'd decided about

her proposition, but with that request her heart thumped in her chest, and something both frightening and hopeful thrummed throughout her body. She wanted to help him feel whole again, though knowing that once she left what they'd intimately shared, he'd be free to do that with other women. Jealousy cramped her stomach. But she'd known from the instant she'd held newborn Rose that she was meant to be a mother. She wanted that with all of her might. She also knew everything in her life came with a cost.

"Okay," was all she managed to get out before he disconnected the call.

She lay back on her beach towel, her face under the umbrella. A whirlwind of hope and desire made it impossible to relax. Anticipation of what might or might not play out later kept her on edge. Knowing from Alexandra the kind of women Wes was used to keeping company with, her one LBD would fall far short of the mark. At least she'd had more time to tan her legs so she wouldn't have to wear stockings to dinner. Hopefully he'd find that sexy enough.

At seven, Mary heard something hit her front door window, like maybe a small bird had flown into it. Since it was more of a thump than a knock, she ignored it and put the finishing touches on her hair and lipstick. She'd worn the one and only little black dress she owned and strappy sandals with lots of fake bling on the straps.

"Harris!"

Why was he yelling for her instead of knocking? She rushed to the door and when she opened it there he was in his huge electric wheelchair on the small plot of grass near where she'd parked her mini house. Several small rocks were on his lap. "Why are you yelling?"

"I tried the old pebbles-on-the-window trick but it didn't work. I didn't want to break your window."

She gave a confused stare.

"Too big for the ramp and it won't fit on your porch. I can't get there to knock." He made a bowing gesture, using only his hands to indicate his wheels. "You look great, by the way."

"Thanks. You're looking pretty good yourself." She opted to play down the fact he looked dashing and scary as hell. Then gave an approving nod after checking out his stylish peach and sage plaid shirt—it complemented his dark eyes—and slim-cut navy blue chinos. Had he been shopping online? "Let me get my purse."

Once she met him on the grass, without another word, he put the electric wheelchair in motion and took off. "Come on, I'm driving."

She had to jog to keep up.

He'd never given her any indication that he was independent enough to drive, yet here he was looking like a guy who did it all the time. What else had he been holding out on her?

They arrived at the three-car garage where someone had already backed out a custom-made candy apple red van. Wes directed Mary to the passenger side and opened the door for her to get in. He steered himself toward the rear hinged doors where he mounted a hydraulic lift, then rolled into place on the driver's side.

"And here I thought you weren't able to get around," she said as he locked himself in. "Turns out you've just been antisocial."

"My prerogative."

"Well, I'm glad you've made the exception for me."

"Don't let it go to your head, Harris. I go to Geoffrey's all the time."

"Since when?"

He acted nonchalant, like they went out to dinner all the time together, definitely making it hard for her to figure out what he'd decided about her offer. Was it too soon to ask?

"Maybe not recently, but I used to be a regular."

Using hand controls and steering knobs, he drove with confidence, even cussed a couple of times when someone cut him off. Within ten minutes they'd arrived at the restaurant, and again she was surprised by the fact the parking attendant seemed to know him. So he had been a regular there BP.

He waited on her side for her to get out of the van and made no effort to hide how he watched her bare legs in the short dress. She was glad she'd painted her toenails bright pink. Was that sexy enough for him?

"Dr. Van Allen, wonderful to see you again,"

the maître d' said, as though nothing monumental had changed about him at all.

The restaurant was able to accommodate his request for a table on the main floor balcony with and a gorgeous view of the ocean. As she relaxed and took everything in, a steward brought wine for Wes to approve—again giving her the impression it was the same wine he always ordered—and Wes ordered an appetizer to share. Like always?

Insecurity put her in competition with any woman he'd ever brought there, and she was suddenly more than a little envious of his prior dates. The thoughts she'd admitted earlier about leaving him, knowing he'd find someone else to fill her place, only ratcheted up the jealous feelings.

"Prawn and scallop ceviche all right with you?"

Snapped out of her thoughts by food, she smiled, hoping she looked more confident than she felt. "Sounds great." She sipped the freshly poured, cool and crisp Sauvignon Blanc. "Wow, this is good."

"It's my personal request whenever I come here."

She'd been right! "So you actually do come here a lot?"

"Not in a while. I brought my parents here after I got the van, but they made such a big deal out of everything I haven't been back since."

"Your parents or the restaurant?"

"Both. I think they got the point when I left abruptly. I called and warned them I was coming and they're doing much better this time. Before the accident, I was a regular on Saturday nights."

She made a note not to make a big deal out of anything, which she'd just been about to do over the full ocean view. *Play it cool. Don't blow it. He may look cool as a cucumber, but he's feeling insecure, too. And my future could be on the line.*

She'd been right. He'd probably been here with loads of women, a new one every week, before the accident. And after she left, the same routine would probably start back up. He'd be working, meeting new people, living a full life. Though that made the green demon rear its ugly head again, in a crazy way it also gave her hope that he'd think nothing of granting her desire to become a mom. With the way things had always been in her life, she couldn't get her hopes up he'd agree to her terms.

"I don't mean to seem eager, but have you made up your mind about what we talked about earlier?" So much for playing it cool. She couldn't help herself.

"Not here, Harris. Let's just have a nice dinner out."

She took his cue and toned it way back. All her hopes and dreams were put on hold while she quaffed light, fruity white wine and enjoyed a chicken roulade she simply couldn't pass up because the spinach bread pudding seemed too interesting to miss. It didn't disappoint.

From time to time, Wes met her gaze, seeming to notice little details about her hair and earrings with his comments. "Between the ocean and those aquamarine earrings, your eyes almost look blue tonight." And another time, "I like how you've done your hair."

Hell, all she'd done was twist it and pile the ends on the top of her head. No biggie. But if he liked it, she was glad she'd gone for something different.

Under any other circumstances—no bartering for sexual favors and pregnancies—she'd have considered tonight a wonderful date with a handsome and bright guy, one she'd hope to go out with again. In or out of a wheelchair.

But this was Wes, the man who needed to prove he was still a man, and she was a soon-to-be thirty-four-year-old who wanted to be a mom with all of her heart—to know how it felt to grow new life inside her body. To give birth to a baby with half of her DNA. *But no pressure.* She fought the urge to blow her wispy bangs off her forehead.

She opted to skip dessert, instead having another glass of wine. Yes, she'd had more than she usually allowed herself, but she wasn't driving and if things went in her favor tonight, she'd be expected to make good on her bargain. Yikes! A little liquid confidence was definitely in order. She took another sip and pretended to watch the sea, knowing Wes was studying her. She chanced a glance his way and found admiring eyes, and a mischievous smile she recalled from his sister's wedding. The night they'd made out like teenagers in the back of the "just married" limousine under the guise of decorating it for the newlyweds. Her face went hot. Dark and sexy thoughts invaded her mind, and feelings like she'd felt when she'd straddled him the other day. So she drank more wine.

"Are you ready to go?"

Maybe once they got home he'd tell her his decision. "Yes," she said, sounding far too eager.

They were oddly quiet the entire drive home, and she chalked it up to the life-changing plans that might or might not be carried out. *Would she be signing a contract tonight?*

Once there, he again asked her to wait so he could help her out of the car. A true and extremely appealing gentleman.

"Come inside with me."

It wasn't a question. And the commanding delivery excited her. She followed, nearly holding her breath.

Rita had left wine chilling in the living room. In all the weeks Mary had been coming to the house, she'd yet to sit in this huge and beautifully furnished room. She sat on the edge of a modern and comfortable couch, so he could roll his wheelchair next to her and serve her another glass of wine. She'd had enough at the restaurant, but sipped to be polite, while he enjoyed his drink. He'd only had one with dinner, no doubt because he was driving. Now they were on his turf, he could relax. And if they were about to have the conversation she hoped they would, maybe he'd need a little something to loosen him up, just like she already had.

Why did she suddenly feel like she needed more?

Surprisingly, they never broached the topic in question for the next hour.

"Remember that time you and Alex snuck Dad's car and came to visit me at UCLA?"

"And we ran out of gas halfway there and had to beg you to come save us? Oh, how could I ever forget? You were so pissed off."

"I was, but I was still glad to see you."

"Could've fooled me. All I remember was you huffing around, scowling, cussing and lecturing us."

"I was worried about you. Both of you. By the way, whose idea was it?"

She went coy, but honestly couldn't remember whose bright idea it had been. "Alex's?"

He obviously liked it when she left him dangling, never knowing for sure if Mary had wanted to see him that night, or if Alex had just wanted to test out her new driving skills. He took her chin between his thumb and index finger.

"Look at me. Tell me it wasn't you."

She tossed her gaze toward the ceiling. "I honestly don't remember."

He'd had his ego stroked enough by that stage in his life, why add to the once but never forgotten Prince of Westwood's inflated pride? Besides, she preferred the humbler man she'd come to know these last several weeks. By far.

Giving up on ever knowing the truth about the UCLA caper, he moved on. So they continued to reminisce about old times, laughing and teasing each other with embarrassing stories. Letting each other know they'd never forgotten the times they'd shared. She decided it was his way to court and woo her, and for his efforts she felt very grateful. The other—the bargain—would feel so cut and dried otherwise.

Out of the blue she leaned over and kissed him. Yes, she'd had another glass of wine and felt bold, but it was more because of how sweet and attentive he'd been over dinner and was continuing to be back home. "Why don't you scoot out of that thing and join me here on the couch?"

He flashed a dashing smile with a hint of danger, his cheeks touched pink from the agreeable wine. "Why didn't I think of that?"

He made the transfer with ease, and she snuggled into him, his hand resting on her thigh, lightly rubbing and kneading her skin.

"So we've got an agreement to discuss."

"That we have," she said, her heart picking up its rhythm at the mere mention of the topic. With his hand on her leg, she already felt he'd staked his claim for his bedroom.

He traced his middle finger from her knee to her upper thigh. "The terms boil down to the proverbial—you scratch my back and I'll scratch yours."

Aside from the fact his finger drove her wild,

the absurd wording made her laugh. *Scratching each other's backs?* "I didn't expect you to get so technical about it."

He joined her laughter. They'd put themselves in an astoundingly awkward position, but neither, so far, had backed out. With his head resting comfortably against the back of the couch next to hers, the last bit of tension seemed to evaporate.

He turned toward her, smiling, watching, making her feel special.

"You know I could pay someone to do what I need, and you could pay a sperm bank, right?"

"True."

"But what would be the fun of that?"

"Also true, but a little scary." She took his hand and squeezed.

"I'm the one who's got the most to prove," he said. "What if you don't get pregnant?"

"Nothing ventured, nothing gained."

His hand broke free and he squeezed the muscles just above her knee. "We seem to be tossing around banal sayings tonight. I hope that isn't an omen for how things go in there." He pointed toward the ceiling, letting her figure out his bedroom was the one upstairs above the living room. Her stomach flip-flopped over the possibility of what might come next.

"So I've made my decision, and I'll accept your bargain under two conditions."

Her head popped off the couch. He'd finally gotten to the good part—helping her have a baby. "Yes? What's that?"

"You move into the house with me, so we can spend the rest of your time here, in Malibu, together."

She should have known he'd never go for such a cold and calculated plan as she'd offered. Honestly, she couldn't imagine how things would actually work out—work out in the morning, sex in the afternoon. Back in the gym the next day.

His compromise was a gentleman's way of making their arrangement personal. Her pulse flittered at the possibility of becoming a bigger part of his life, which made her feel extremely turned on. This was her chance to finally get to know

Wesley Van Allen in a way she'd only dreamed of before. Who needed to think about that?

"And if you get pregnant, I want to be the dad. A real dad."

She almost slid off the couch. "You mean like sharing the responsibility? That's exactly what I promised you wouldn't happen."

"I couldn't live with myself otherwise."

"But we won't be together."

"And I don't want to be written out of my child's life."

"We don't even know if I'll get pregnant."

"Or that I can actually have sex."

"True. Maybe we should quit talking."

"Less talk, more action?"

They laughed, realizing they'd resorted to yet another cliché.

"It's a deal."

Obviously happy, he leaned into her and they kissed. Soon passion heated the way, their kisses growing frantic, his hand, which shifted from her knee to the inside of her thigh, sending a thrill straight to her core. As he delved deeper with his mouth, hers welcoming him, his fingers found a way beneath the lace of her underwear, and soon their make-out session took on a whole new dynamic.

And Wes knew exactly how to make this woman like putty in his hands.

CHAPTER EIGHT

AN HOUR LATER, Wes had proof the brain was definitely the biggest sex organ. Seeing Mary naked, knowing he'd made her come using his hands and his mouth, seeing how she still wanted him until they'd joined together, made every worry evaporate. He was a man who wanted a woman, and by some magic she'd shared with him he'd made love to her. Completely.

That paraplegic girlfriend blogger had been right. The sex had been gratifying in ways he'd never imagined, and Mary had been the number one secret ingredient. He'd thought he'd known her body from working out with her every day with her wearing skimpy workout shorts and tops. But seeing her nude, feeling every inch of her satin skin, tasting her, inhaling her special scent, discovering what she liked and what she *really* liked, had been completely different from what he'd imagined. Damn, she was gorgeous, and sexy, and he'd sent her over the edge. Him, a guy who couldn't use his legs or hips.

She'd also made him feel something he'd never thought he'd feel again. When she'd orgasmed over him, he could have sworn he'd felt her tightening around him—whether it was his imagination or had been real didn't matter because he'd "felt" it, thanks to that huge sex organ called his brain—and he'd been as hot with desire as he'd ever been. That last special sensation of her rhythmically gripping him as she'd come had sent a message shooting straight up his spine. There was no denying that part. Then she'd assured him that he'd ejaculated.

He'd never expected anything like that to ever happen again. Not because it wasn't possible but because he'd snobbishly assumed it would never be good enough, so why settle or even try?

Now they snuggled in his bed and, closing his eyes, holding and feeling her next to him, breathing his scent all over her, he remembered what a major part of being a man was. He'd made her his, and she'd willingly given him all she had. Nothing in the world felt better than that.

He smiled into the darkness, stroking her shoulder as she curled into him.

"That was nothing short of amazing," she whispered.

To hell with being humble. He'd done it for her, and she'd just told him it had been amazing. Yeah, that definitely got a grin out of him.

Mary couldn't believe the way this day had wound up. She'd been bold enough to state her case and ask the most brilliant man she knew to father a baby with her—a guy who wasn't sure if he'd ever have another intimate relationship again—and now she'd had the most astounding experience in her life.

They'd always had sexual chemistry, had just never acted on it. Well, never completely acted on it, though they'd come pretty darn close at Alexandra's wedding.

The important thing now was to keep her head on tight, not let her thoughts float up to the rainbow-colored clouds that seemed to have appeared since Wes had said yes. Though he'd thrown her a curveball about wanting to be actively involved as her baby's father; that was, if she actually got pregnant. She felt closer to him than she'd ever dreamed and realized she was in a precarious position. She'd helped him prove he could still be sexually active, which was great, but the down side was she'd have to leave soon, and now that he knew he could, a man like him would easily find someone else to carry on with.

Jealousy threaded around her heart again, as it had so many times already that day.

Why hadn't she thought about that part of the deal when she'd gotten her bright idea about him fathering her child the old-fashioned way? Or his insisting he'd want to stay a part of her life if she got pregnant.

Suddenly a seemingly straightforward plan had gotten surprisingly complicated. Maybe they should forget the whole thing.

Too late. Things had changed between them now, in a major way. For the next few weeks it would be up to her to make sure the main reason she'd come to Malibu stayed in focus. To help Wes step back into his old life.

He lay beside her, a contented expression on his face, the most relaxed she'd ever seen him. She put her chin on her hands that rested on his chest, and studied him.

"What?" he said.

No way could she let him know her true thoughts. That she loved being here with him. That in a sense it had been a dream come true. Boy, if she could only talk to her fifteen-year-old self right now—*Just wait, one day you'll be with him*. She chuckled inside, and hoped he couldn't read her mind from her delirious expressions. But being with Wes was so much more than that. The portion of life they'd staked out together in his gym had come to mean more than she'd ever hoped. Especially now. And she needed to put the kibosh on these useless, fanciful thoughts. "Don't expect this to get you a free pass in the gym tomorrow."

"Slave driver." He tightened his grip around her and kissed her forehead. They definitely had something good going on.

And coming to Malibu to help an old friend could be the most dangerous thing she'd ever done in her life.

Of all times for Alexandra to call! Wes had sent Mary home early to pack up and move in with him. At least she didn't have to lie when Alex asked what she was up to.

"Just doing some straightening up around the house." She used a damp paper towel from the kitchen and mindlessly wiped up dust on the counter in the kitchen so as not to be a liar.

"Your house. Yes, that's right, your tiny house. How's that going?"

"Great. Remember I sent you some photos when I first bought it?" Two years ago.

"Vaguely. I'd assumed you'd be living in the house with Wes."

Was she a mind reader? "Why do that when I've got my lovely little house, and all that privacy?"

"I guess you've got a point, but he's got that gorgeous estate. But, oh, hey, I'll get to see your house tomorrow in person."

"Tomorrow?" Mary's casual cleaning motions quickly turned into a tornado of wiping and scrubbing.

"Yes. I've just gotten off the phone with Wes and told him my plane arrives tomorrow at nine. Will you come get me?"

She glanced at her phone, only then seeing the text slide in from Wes—*Alex is coming!*

"Of course. Can't wait to see you! How great. It'll be like old times with the three of us together." And no more "hot" nights with Wes until after Alex left, even though Mary was entering her ovulation period. "How long are you planning to stay?"

"A couple of days."

Damn! "That's wonderful." Mary hoped she'd kept a cheerful tone in her voice, even though Alex's visit would seriously mess with her and Wes's plans. Between the sheets!

Adjusting her attitude, Mary remembered Alex was, after all, her best friend for life, but her showing up at this crucial time of their bargain—and her cycle—would be challenging to say the least. She'd need to keep a poker face where Wes was concerned, but how could she hide her true feelings from her best friend? Freaking over the moon with the chance to get pregnant by the guy she'd had a crush on since she was fifteen, and now that guy had become the man who'd blown the roof off her sex life on their first encounter.

"How's my brother doing?" Alex asked, in a decidedly serious tone.

Mary suppressed her cough. "Well. He's doing well. Made a lot of progress." Boy, had he ever! Did she mention he'd blown her mind sexually last night and had given her an incredible wake-up call just an hour ago? Not to Alex, she wouldn't!

"Mommy, Mommy." Two tiny voices demanded their mother's attention.

"I'm going to have to go now. You'll have to tell me all about Wes's progress on the ride from the airport tomorrow."

"Are you bringing Rose?" Even now, frantic and surprised, Mary wanted a chance to hold that toddler who'd turned her world upside down the day she'd been born.

"Not this trip. You'll have to come here soon. Promise?"

"Mommy!"

"That's a promise."

"I can't wait to see both of you."

"Me too! I'll meet you at baggage claim tomorrow."

Mary disconnected the call and closed her overnight case, since it would be a waste of time to pack it now. Her moving in with Alexandra's big brother would have to wait a few more days, until after she'd gone.

The next afternoon, Rita had put together a lovely spread of appetizers. Wes, Alexandra and Mary sat on the front patio, all taking in the sun, drinking sangria and snacking.

"I've never seen you look so relaxed, Wes. I think Mary is a good influence on you." Alex tucked her nearly black hair behind one ear. She wore it stylishly straight at chin length with Cleopatra bangs and looked much younger than thirty-five, especially with the midnight-blue highlights. Her long, narrow nose and coffee-brown eyes, so similar to her brother's, gave nothing away if she was by any chance suspicious about why her brother was so relaxed.

"We've gotten into a good routine, that's for sure."

Mary nearly spewed her drink over Wes's loaded response, but coughed and choked instead.

"You okay?" Alexandra tapped Mary's back a few times until she settled down.

"Went down the wrong way." She glanced at Wes, that mischievous glint in his eyes sparkling in the sun, and sent him a warning, though stealthy glare, then quickly looked away.

He popped a shrimp into his mouth and chewed vigorously. "We'll have to show you the gym later. This crazy lady has me cycling and doing gymnastics workouts."

"Well, you've never looked fitter."

"He's also thinking about going back to work again soon, right?"

She'd caught him off guard, and it showed by the way he stopped reaching for the avocado dip. "Yes. I guess I am. Gonna get measured for this special wheelchair that can help me stand for surgery."

"Wow, that's fantastic."

"I almost couldn't believe it when he showed me the video of the doctor doing surgery in this futuristic-looking contraption," Mary said.

"I knew I'd done the right thing, begging you to come."

"Oh, we had a rocky start, but Wes is a reasonable guy." *And a maniac in the bedroom!*

Alex started giggling. "Oh, gosh, remember that time I stole my Dad's car and we went to see Wes, but ran out of gas first?"

They all laughed, Mary and Wes more so because they'd just been talking about that last night, BS—before sex.

"How could I forget?" he said. "So whose idea was it anyway?"

Mary's eyes went wide. Damn.

"Mary's, of course. Come on, you must have known about her huge crush on you back then."

A Cheshire cat grin accompanied the "busted" stare coming from Wes. Her ears went hot.

Over the two days of Alexandra's visit Mary

and Wes passed meaningful, though surreptitious looks when they all went to the movies that first night. Another thing Mary hadn't realized Wes still liked to do. And after Alex and Mary had gone to the beach the next afternoon, Wes met them at the hot tub for a long and relaxing group soak.

Dying to be with him, Mary found ways to touch him, and he did the same. "Oh, excuse me," he'd say, after reaching across her and grabbing a sneaky squeeze on her thigh. His mere touch set off a path of thrills straight to her center. Or she'd lean over him, managing to brush her chest against his while reaching for a spa towel. When Alex wasn't around, they'd grab quick kisses, filled with excitement and promises for make-up time soon. She'd done a lot of clenching by the end of day two.

"You haven't seen my house yet. Come, let me show you," she said to Alexandra, mainly to break up the torture of being so near yet so far from Wes.

"Yes. I'm dying to see how you manage there."

Once Mary had given her introductory tour,

and Alex had given the obligatory compliments along the way, she nailed Mary with a no-nonsense stare.

“What’s going between you and my brother?”

“Is it that obvious?”

“I almost didn’t know where to look watching the two of you make love with your eyes over the dinner table last night!”

Mary felt heat rise all the way to the crown of her head. “It’s not what you think.”

“I think it’s definitely what I think. Now, are you going to tell me or do I have to ask him?”

Mortified that Alex actually would go to her brother, Mary spilled some of the facts but left out the part about everything starting with a bargain.

“I knew you guys always had chemistry. Pity it took his accident to finally bring you together,” Alex said with tears brightening her eyes.

“In a way, getting to know Wes has been healing for me.”

“And for him! My God, his attitude used to be unbearable. Now he seems like his old self again." She took Mary's hands and squeezed. "I can't thank you enough."

How should she respond? *It's just part of my job?* "Like I said, we're healing each other."

Later, it was time to say goodbye to her brother. "Something told me Mary was the only person who could help you. I'm so glad you've found each other."

He looked perplexed, but accepted her good wishes. It seemed Mary held her breath until Alex was finally gone and she and Wesley were alone again. Turned out to be for a good reason, too. Because he'd shut down a little. And had withdrawn.

Had letting his sister know something was going on between them ruined what they'd salvaged from their relationship? Had her stepping over the line with her bold bargain proved to be nothing more than craziness?

Mary shook her head, her face dropping into her hands. How badly had she screwed things up?

Wes worked like a fiend in the gym over the next few days, and as he did so he remembered all the things Mary had said to him about picking up his old life again and working as a doctor. Because of her, he wanted to live each day to the best of his ability and believed he could once again achieve a life he actually enjoyed. Just different. She'd believed in him when he'd given up. He'd gotten sick of feeling like a victim anyway.

Why should he be uncomfortable with his sister knowing he and Mary had become lovers? Why hold that against Mary? It didn't make sense, and he certainly hadn't stopped having sex with her because of it, he'd just held back some of the confusing feelings that arose along with the great sex. He was sure Mary sensed him pulling back, too. Ah, hell, what was the point of overthinking their bargain? Enjoy it while it lasted. It would take a miracle for her to get pregnant. He pushed the negative thoughts away. Wasn't it time to seize the day again?

"You're going to injure yourself if you keep up those repetitions with that amount of weight," she said, chiding him, but the expression on her face said otherwise. He'd impressed her, he knew it and he liked it.

"I could go on all day."

The light touch of her fingers tickled across his neck. "Save some of that energy for later."

Thanks to the devices he'd ordered to help make intimacy easier and more satisfying, their last few days had gone by in a crazy sexy haze as they tried them out. Making up for the lost time during Alexandra's visit, he'd wanted her often, and she'd complied. So different from Giselle, Mary seemed perfect for him.

He couldn't fool himself into thinking it was totally him. He understood she had an ulterior motive, and the fact was her fertility cycle ruled the day. Still, lucky him.

Following her PT regimen had made him stronger than ever, after having reached a plateau with his own workout before she'd arrived. Wasn't that what she'd promised? Give her two months—that was how she'd tried to sell her brand of healing.

He finished another set of repetitions, thinking the upper half of his body had never been stronger. His thoughts circled back to Mary. A disturbing thought popped into his head. Was he falling in love? Then another—was he even capable of being a father?

She'd be leaving soon, and he needed to get on with life, not get stuck in a rut of wanting someone he'd never have. "I'm going to call the head of neurosurgery this afternoon to let him know I'm ready to come back to work."

She wasn't able to hide the surprise, and he saw it clearly in those ocean-green eyes. "They'll be thrilled to have you, too." *Great cover, Harris.* The fact she'd poorly hidden one moment of… what, sadness, fear, loss, encouraged him that she might have feelings for him, too.

He grabbed her and pulled her onto his lap. "Thought I'd venture back a little at a time. See some patients. Watch some surgery. See where that leads."

"Order that special stand-up wheelchair now." She'd clicked into PT mode. All business. Was that her defense?

"I already have."

"Someone will need to come and measure. Who knows how long it takes to make one."

"That's been arranged too, Harris. Besides,

going back to work sooner or later doesn't matter, just as long as I get there." He'd surprised her again, going all Zen. He'd surprised himself, too.

"This from the impatient man I found in your gym six weeks ago?"

"You've changed me. I give credit where it's due."

She hugged him. "Thank you. But you've done all the hard work."

"That's because I've had a relentless slave driver as a coach."

His face was close enough to see flecks of gold in the kaleidoscope of green and amber in her irises. He'd miss those eyes. Overcome with feelings he wasn't ready to sort out, he kissed her, his mouth melding with the lips he'd come to want and need more than he'd ever imagined possible. She'd fought her way back into his life, and now had conquered him. He opened the kiss and plunged his tongue inside in a desperate move. She matched his urgency, pressing her body tight against his chest. His hands roamed her back and hips as if he'd never touched her before, frantic to find what he needed. Her. All of her. She rocked over his lap, taking his breath with her kisses, and he knew he'd found home.

Whoever had designed that glider chair and the cot with extra bounce was a flat-out genius. Mary plopped back on the cot completely sated. Wes had so much upper body strength he'd stayed on top as she'd utilized the rebound of the special fabric beneath, her legs wrapped around his waist as the cot enhanced their timing, moving them piston-quick. When his strength faltered briefly, her arms held him where she needed for those last crucial seconds. Wow, had that been worth it. What teamwork! Though on her back, she'd controlled the rate and rhythm, and when Wes had once again held strong in a push-up above her, she'd gone for it and had quickly found her golden ticket to heaven.

He'd started reacting to her orgasms as if they were his own, and she believed he felt what she felt, just in his own way.

Now that she'd settled down, he collapsed beside her. Still unable to talk, all she could do was shake her head. *Wow! Just wow.* He gave his self-satisfied look, which she loved, but pretended otherwise.

"This is crazy," she said after several more seconds of basking in the post-sex haze.

"Not nearly crazy enough."

Her head bobbed up. "You're already tired of me? Am I going to have to do that impossible position from that horrible porn movie?"

"No way. I'm just saying I'm happy to oblige, no matter how often."

"With all the times we've been together, I'll be shocked if—" Damn, she hadn't meant to bring the passion they'd just shared down to the mere function of a bargain they'd made. *Get me pregnant. That's the point of all this.*

Because it wasn't. Not anymore.

"Don't get your hopes up too much," he said, breaking into her thoughts. "I've been reading up on this and apparently paraplegic sperm motility isn't always up to par."

Funny he hadn't mentioned that before now, after two full weeks of mating like bunnies. "All it takes is one good swimmer."

He spanked her once and pulled her closer on top of him. “Then here’s to one good swimmer.”

He kissed the top of her head, and for some reason that chaste and tender kiss felt more special than all the fiery ones that had preceded it, sending a cascade of tingles down her neck and fanning over her shoulders.

Wesley Van Allen held the magic touch for Mary…but their days together were numbered.

Two days later Mary assisted Wes with passive range of motion to warm up. His hips, knees and ankle joints were flexible and healthy, and she’d managed to stop the progression of atrophy of his leg muscles. But the credit wasn’t all hers. “Okay, onto the bike.”

“Yes, boss.”

Using his superb upper body strength, he shifted from the workout wheelchair onto the stationary bike designed especially for paraplegics. In her quest to help Wesley live a long, vital life, she knew from the beginning his circulation had to be addressed. Since money was no object with him, shortly after she’d come to help, she’d ordered the amazing stationary bicycle designed especially for him.

Since its arrival a month ago, they'd utilized the bike as part of his daily routine. She strapped his right leg in the holder and his foot to the pedal. He insisted on doing the same for the left leg. Next, she attached electrodes to his right thigh and gluteus maximus muscles.

"Here, let me do that," he said, setting himself up on the left side. She intended to flip on the switch on the control panel, but he stopped her. So she stood back and let him set up the bike for his proper daily workout. He chose the high-intensity mode, which involved four minutes of hard exercise with an equal interval of easier training. Four sets.

He knew as well as she did that this exercise demanded energy that increased his blood flow and pulse, with the benefit of accelerating oxygen uptake and enhancing the heart's pumping volume. Once he'd read the Norwegian university study on this very subject, he'd become a believer. This style of aerobic exercise would add years to his life. And if Mary miraculously got pregnant, she'd want the father of her baby to hang around for a long time. All for the baby's sake, of course.

"Remember to check on that order for the arm cycle," he said during the second repetition, hardly winded. "When I go back to work I won't have time to spend hours in the gym."

That was a fact. He'd need exercises that maximized the workout in minimal time. Using the bike, along with a similar contraption for his arms, would buy him precious time as well as multiple physical benefits.

As she watched him tear up the imaginary road on his bike, one more thought came flying at her and landed right between her eyes. He didn't need her anymore. She'd come to help get him back on track, and now he'd taken off at a sprint on his own. Her job here was done.

Then another thought landed, this one weighing heavily on her mind. The fact that she'd accepted her next assignment and would have to leave for Astoria, Oregon, in another week. Was she ready to say goodbye to Wes? More importantly, would she ever know if he felt the same way about her as she did about him?

She'd made the biggest mistake of her life and had fallen in love with him. That old insecurity of her teens had her thinking that if she dared to stay, he wouldn't want her, and she was afraid to find out.

Chuck had left because, after all they'd shared between them, she hadn't made the grade. It had cut her to the core, having opened her heart to love, only to have it tossed aside as her lover had set off for parts unknown. Why would she think a man like Wes, the once Prince of Westwood, a brain doctor, who knew where she'd come from—had seen the trailer park first hand—would ever see her as an equal, or good enough to love?

No, it was better to leave things as they were, he going back to work and she, well, just going. But if she was lucky, she'd be taking something special along with her. A part of Wes. His baby.

The Prince of Westwood had granted her that wish. And she'd certainly lived up to her part of the bargain. The guy was an amazing lover. He'd also said he wanted to get involved with the baby's life if the unlikely occurred, which would be tricky if they lived in different states. But she wouldn't deprive him of that. Maybe she should find a job and settle down here.

A baby *and* a relationship with Wes was too much to hope for. Wasn't it?

Three days later, Mary began packing up the house and hoped she'd be prepared for her thousand-plus-mile drive to her next job in Astoria by the weekend. When she'd first arrived nearly two months ago, she hadn't expected leaving to be so hard. She'd broken a professional cardinal rule, never to fall for a patient. Up until now that had never been a problem, no matter how cute some of them had been.

But she and Wes had set things up differently. She hadn't been employed by Wes—she'd come as an old friend. He might not have considered her a friend at the time, but they'd worked through their differences and had quickly skipped from friends to lovers. Who had time to fall in love? Yet she had. Her bargain, an offer that only a true friend would make to a man like Wes—to help him understand he could still have sex—had turned out to be a huge mistake.

What had made her think she could keep their lovemaking clinical? He'd needed something. She'd needed something. It had made sense at the time. Now she was left with a wadded-up mess of love clogging her heart.

Hell, they'd used each other, and while thinking how civilized she was, she'd accidentally fallen in love. Stupid. Stupid. Stupid. She could only speak for herself, of course, but from the way Wesley seemed to be moping around these last couple of days, she suspected he might have his regrets, too.

What could have been a disastrous attempt to help him understand that sex was doable as a paraplegic had turned into a profound experience, one that had changed her life forever, too.

And there he was, at her tiny house door, the man she could never admit her true feelings to because he had far too much on his plate already. And her chest squeezed with that unique sensation she wasn't supposed to feel.

"I've been thinking, Harris."

"Oh, that's always dangerous." She gave her best shot at being upbeat and fun.

He gave a tolerant smile, watching her with warm brown benevolent eyes. "I've been thinking you should look for a job closer by so we can keep in touch. See each other."

She nearly lost her balance, but blamed it on the cardboard box underfoot, then recovered as quickly as she could.

Wes understood Mary fiercely needed her independence, and she'd never settle for only being a live-in girlfriend, catering to him and him alone. Sure, it was a nice fantasy, but one that would never work. Under those circumstances, he'd soon lose respect for her, as she would for him. Yet that was all he really had to offer her. She'd be miserable, strapped down with him. So the next best thing would be for her to work in Los Angeles. And the best way for him to convince her that she wouldn't be completely trapped in a life with him was to show her he could live a regular life. Wasn't that what she'd been hammering home since she'd gotten here?

"I know you're busy packing, but let's take the

day off tomorrow and go to the Getty Museum. There's a smaller one right down the road in Pacific Palisades, the Getty Villa."

Surprise brightened her face and the sweetest unassuming smile followed. "I could use a break." She gestured to the several cartons and boxes lining her mini living room. "I'd love to."

"Great, I'll order some tickets online right now."

Once he'd used his phone to secure entrance to the museum the next day, he stuck around. The least a man could do was help her with her packing, so they spent the rest of the afternoon putting her dishes in boxes and securing anything else that could break in drawers and inside the tiniest closets he'd ever seen.

"What about the bed?" Yeah, he was a guy, always thinking about beds. Especially where Mary was concerned.

"That's pretty much secured up there, but I still put up a plywood barrier to keep the dresser from sliding around. Oh, that reminds me, I need to pack away the mirror from up there."

She had a mirror in her bedroom? Hmm, that

sounded promising. Yet he'd never get to see the bed or the mirror since the only way to her loft was up a narrow ladder. *Paraplegic stopped by climbing device.* The metaphor of not being able to make it over that never-ending hill AP—after paraplegia—seemed especially appropriate for their situation. He'd also been hit with a wave of claustrophobia like the first time he'd come to visit, so he thought up a reasonable excuse and made a quick exit.

The next day, he displayed all his independent skills by driving, parking, and using his electric wheelchair to get around the Roman-styled architecture of the museum. As they strolled along the side of the main Grecian-styled pool and the central courtyard gardens, and later the gallery within the villa, he didn't notice a single sculpture. Instead, he spent the entire afternoon admiring her. How her strawberry blonde hair brushed her face when she turned too quickly. How she pursed her lips when she concentrated while using earbuds and the self-guided tour to study the collections. How delicate her hands were, even though she could pump iron with the best of them. How she glanced at him often, making sure he was enjoying the Greek and Roman antiquities as much as she was. He fudged and pretended he was.

She was his museum, the person who knew his past, who was the one woman who had seen him completely vulnerable in all his paralyzed glory, yet who'd still seen something worth wanting in him. With her around, he felt confident and alive. He could see his future. The question was, how would he get along without her?

He had to. Otherwise all her efforts would be for naught and she'd have failed. He owed her his success. And so much more. She'd reawakened his sleeping soul. She'd showed him step by step how to flourish. He'd even learned a magic trick or two thanks to her unorthodox approach to rehab for fine motor skills. But most of all, with her PT regimen, she'd ensured he'd have a long and healthy life as a paraplegic. He couldn't let her down.

He'd go back to work and pick up where he'd

left off. He'd already ordered the special stand-up wheelchair, and expected to be doing neurosurgery again within the next few months. He'd prove to her, his family and the world he could go on, and quit hiding out in his comfortable cave. He'd join the living again and make a life for himself. That was the only way he knew how to repay her.

"I'm done," she said, clicking off the self-guided tour and removing the headphones.

"Did you enjoy it?"

"Totally. I'd like to come here again sometime."

"I'd be happy to bring you. Just say when."

She caught his gaze and he thought he saw a hint of longing in hers but knew he'd probably read into that look out of wishful thinking.

Instead of replying, she took his hand and squeezed. All the answer he needed.

"I thought we could have an early dinner out, if you'd like?"

She glanced around thoughtfully, as if searching for the best way to say what she needed. "You know what I'd like? To go back to Malibu and cook dinner for you. I've been here almost two months and only cooked for you once."

"If that's what you want."

"You'll be dessert." She winked and walked ahead, leaving him grinning and forgetting to push the forward button on his chair.

CHAPTER NINE

HOURS LATER, AFTER Mary had prepared a simple meal of chicken in lemon and herb sauce, quinoa and salad, because that was what he had handy in his kitchen, they took a stroll on the beach. He used his workout wheelchair that rolled easily along the wet, packed-down low-tide sand, like a bicycle would have.

The chill of the night had Mary hugging herself, but she didn't complain. The lapis lazuli sky was thick with stars, and frothy fluorescence-tipped waves rolled one after another to shore. Wes had to move quickly to avoid getting his chair wet more than a few times. But they carried on because the ocean always brought peace, and Wes needed peace of mind with that damned ticking clock hanging over his head, and the barrage of thoughts plaguing him. The foremost was that Mary would be leaving soon.

Back at his house, Wes took Mary's hand and kissed it. "Come with me." He pulled her along the path to his porch, across his living room and into his private elevator. When the doors closed he grasped her hips and tugged her near, hugging her tight around the waist and resting his head on her breasts. "I've wanted you all day."

She ran her fingers over his freshly buzzed hair. "You must have read my mind."

Once in his bedroom, fighting the passion that threatened to take over, he helped her undress, taking time to lightly stroke and touch her skin as the layers of clothing came off, rather than ravish her as he longed to. When he removed her bra he tasted the velvet of each tip as she tensed and swayed under the touch of his mouth. His mind swirled with hunger for more, yet he held back, instead settling for the sensation of the bud as it peaked against his tongue.

He edged her onto the bed, spreading her legs, running his fingers over the satin-smooth skin of the inside of her thighs, then leaned forward, mesmerized by her heady scent. He covered her with his mouth, at first only flicking his tongue, teasing her, hunting for that tiny nub, then using long strokes to soothe her into submission. She let loose a long quivery sigh. Her sweet taste made him feel drunk with desire. She purred for him, and he kept her floating in that special state of bliss for as long as she'd let him. This was all about her, and his need to show how much he wanted to make her happy. Hoping she'd never forget him.

Soon she arched her back and he delved deeper and flattened his tongue, rubbing and licking, enjoying the whimpering sounds and squirming under his touch. He clutched her bottom and went deep, bringing her to the brink then pushing her over with a cadence of stiff strokes and one endless swirl. She gasped and her belly quaked. Unrelenting, he drove her to bucking and crying out, until she'd gone completely, lost to his wizardry. And even then he hadn't begun to come close to showing her the depth of how much he needed her.

* * *

Morning broke through the edges of the window and Mary tried to open her eyes to the glare.

"What time is it?" She sat up, searching for the nearest bedside clock.

Wesley slept peacefully beside her. They'd made love like the world had been ending last night, and she was sore to prove it, but in a wonderfully contented way. She stroked his cheek and he began a long, meandering journey toward waking up. Then it hit her. She was leaving in two days. She'd never have the chance to see him like this again, and her chest gripped like a vise.

His eyes now opened, obviously not having clicked in with the living quite yet, Wes smiled sleepily and blissfully at her. She wanted with all of her being to stay with him, wished it was possible, but knew better. If he realized how much she wanted him in her life, he might think she'd trapped him with a baby bargain. Why further complicate his life with her mistake of falling in love?

They'd risked it all with that crazy bargain—first proving he could have satisfying sex again, and, boy, oh, boy, had they proved that beyond any doubt, and, second, trying to get her pregnant. Well, half of the bargain was better than nothing. And life would be far less complicated this way.

"Let's skip the gym workout today and stay right here," he said, stroking her arm.

It would be so easy to do that, to get lost in his body, to hold him close, but she might never want to let him go and, worse yet, she might tell him how she really felt.

That wouldn't be fair, and would be far beyond what he'd bargained for. He'd call it sabotage. She couldn't do that to Wes, not when his life was just beginning to get back on track.

"Sounds great, but to make up for taking yesterday off, I've got to finish up my packing. And don't you have a meeting with the head of neurosurgery later?"

"Ah, damn, yes. But that's not until noon. Let's stay here a little longer, at least."

She couldn't get lured into making love with him again. After last night, giving him everything she'd had, and he still hadn't uttered a word about loving her, she needed to start protecting herself. It would be hard enough to leave. Why set herself up to rip out an even bigger piece of her heart? No. She had to toughen up, accept that where men were concerned she'd yet to measure up. First with Chuck, who'd walked away from her, and now with Wes, who was letting her leave. Yeah, she needed to harden her heart, and it may as well begin right now.

"I'm pretty sure I've met my end of the bargain. I proved you could have sex. Great sex, may I remind you."

He grabbed her hip and rolled her closer. "Since we're talking about our bargain, then your half hasn't been met. I promised to make you pregnant. I don't think you should leave until we've achieved that goal."

She laughed with him, keeping things light yet seeing something careful going on behind his casual mask. *Oh, yes, aren't we so grown up and worldly with our bargain.* "Theoretically, that sounds great, but I hate to remind you I've got a new job to start on Monday, and it's going to take me the weekend to drive to Oregon."

She was probably reading into his look, but she could have sworn she saw panic flash inside those caramel-tinted dreamy eyes. “All the more reason to take the morning off. Let’s give it one last try. I owe you. Right?”

It certainly wasn’t a flowery proposition, but he was being honest. She wanted a baby, had risked her heart for it, so shouldn’t she do whatever it took to know she’d done her best? Taking cold, hard logic into consideration, how could she refuse?

She moved into his open arms, loving the heat of his body and the feeling of home she’d recently found in his embrace. Maybe this time he’d admit how he really felt about her. Should she be the first to say the L word?

Mary had been wrong. Yes, they’d made love like they hadn’t seen each other in weeks, but Wes hadn’t confessed any special feelings for her beyond, “Wow, was that as good for you as it was for me?”

She’d let herself down, too, by not having the guts to tell him how she felt. What was the use?

She was leaving. Telling him she loved him would ruin everything they'd worked so hard on the last two months. All it would do was prove to Wes that he should never have let her in his house in the first place. Damn, she'd fouled up.

They weren't meant to be together, or they would have taken that chance ten years ago, at his sister's wedding. Everything had been perfect then. She could have taken a job near him as he hadn't yet been officially engaged. The timing had been perfect. Yet they hadn't even had the nerve to find out what it would be like to have sex. That said it all, didn't it? And things were so, so different now.

She had a life to go back to. Her own little home. He was still picking up the pieces of his, but it was a start, and his future, once again, looked bright.

"Just to let you know, I'll be sleeping at my place tonight," she said, beginning her exit strategy, if she could call it that. Because she was nowhere near ready to say goodbye to Wesley Van Allen. "I want to get an early start on the road, and—"

"Wait a minute. What? You're leaving tomorrow? I thought—"

"I've changed my mind. I'd like to get there a day early so I can set up my house and be ready to start the job full out on Monday."

He shook his head, not looking in the least bit pleased. "I've got this meeting this afternoon, and you're messing with my concentration. Can't you leave on Saturday, like you originally said?"

She let hurt and an aching heart speak unedited for her. "It's not always all about you, Wesley. Sorry, I can't accommodate you this time."

She turned to leave his bedroom, after having taken only a minute to put on her clothes.

"Harris, that's not what I meant."

Too late. Instead of looking back, she strode to the door, knowing he couldn't catch her.

Mary stood her ground and refused to rush back to Wes that night. He owed her an apology. But he hadn't come crawling to her door, like she'd expected. Beyond the argument, she'd been dying to hear how his meeting had gone, but figured if he wanted her to know, he'd come and tell her.

It turned out he was as stubborn as she was, but she already knew that. So why did it hurt so much?

As she lay in her loft, still angry but realizing she could have spent one last night with Wes if she hadn't gone all emotional and let hurt do her talking, she broke down. Feeling raw, hormonal and completely mixed up, she cried until her eyes swelled shut.

Her gut assured her she really never had been good enough for him. Even now, with their playing field somewhat leveled. Because he was still rich. He'd been raised like a prince, the Prince of Westwood—it was in his blood to be proud. In his parents' eyes, the universe truly did revolve around him. They'd convinced him of it, too. She'd come from a trailer park, not one of those upscale versions around these days but the last-ditch, park-what-you've-got kind of place. Starting humble like that, everything else was a step up. Now she lived like a vagabond, traveling around the country in her tiny portable house. Owning that house was the best she could do for herself and, damn it, she was proud of what she'd accomplished after starting from nothing. And yet she still didn't feel good enough for Wes.

He'd sat there stoically in his bed, like the world owed him something, like she owed him something. Her early departure hadn't worked for his timeline. Seriously? Well, to hell with him!

But she loved him. Damn it. She picked up her cellphone and brought up his number, ready to call and tell him everything she felt. Why not? She was leaving. Say it and go. Let him figure out the rest. But the next second she stopped and, chickening out, she never pressed "call".

The next morning, after several rounds of cold compresses on her eyes, feeling she finally looked decent enough to face him without giving herself away, she set out to say goodbye. And pride be damned, a swarm of butterflies seemed to take over her stomach.

Wes had hardly slept. His meeting at the hospital had gone well, and he'd be returning to work in two weeks, but the way things had been left with Mary yesterday morning had nagged at his peace of mind all night. She'd acted out of character, surprising him about leaving early, then had gotten all moody and snide when he'd blundered his immediate response. He'd given a knee-jerk reaction and an equally adolescent reply—"You're messing with my concentration. Can't you leave on Saturday?" Good Lord, what an ass. It had come off like a hurt child taking his toys and going home.

In other words, he'd blown it. Big time. He should have apologized on the spot, but his damn pride had tripped him up and, having a deep grasp on him, that same pride had kept him from going to see her last night. Instead, he'd waited for her to come to her senses.

And he considered himself a fairly well-adjusted adult, how?

Today he'd woken up with a double helping of remorse, but couldn't for the life of him figure out how to make things right. Though he knew one thing, he needed to go to her and apologize.

In the kitchen, Wes put together something to eat. His stomach was in knots and he wasn't even sure he'd be able to get anything down. Then the doorbell rang. Over the last two months, Mary had made herself at home, coming and going any time she wanted. He'd made a point to leave the door unlocked for her today, too.

But the doorbell rang again.

He wheeled himself to answer, wondering if it might be someone else, but there she stood, looking beautiful and heartbreakingly sad.

"I'm all packed and ready to go," she said. Her hair pulled back in a ponytail, without a stitch of makeup on, wearing cut-off jeans and an old T-shirt, she looked like he remembered her at fifteen. He detected some puffiness around her eyes, and they looked far less clear than usual. Knowing he'd been responsible for that made his gut twist tighter.

"Come in. Don't stay on the doorstep. Let's have a proper goodbye." He moved back, making room for her. She hesitated, then cautiously stepped inside.

He tugged her hand and pulled her close, wanting nothing more than to kiss her. She resisted. So he bussed her cheek. No, they couldn't separate under these circumstances. "What have I done, Harris? I apologize for being a jerk yesterday, okay? Why are you acting this way?"

She shook her head. "You haven't done anything, Wes."

Why did he get the distinct feeling there was a whole lot more to that answer? "Yes, I have. I've made you angry, and I can't stand you leaving under these circumstances."

She studied her feet. "Well, it's not like we have the gift of time to work things out, right?"

For a lady who always named the elephant in the room, she was sure dodging the issue. Since he might never see her again, he needed to say what he'd been thinking all night, beyond giving an apology. "I know we agreed to use each other, but this leaving on such bad terms seems so cold."

"Use each other?"

Damn, he'd chosen the wrong words again. "You know what I mean."

"We made a bargain."

"Yes." Sadness enveloped him, topped off with old anger that still managed to trip him up when he wasn't careful. "I foolishly thought we actually had something." A devastating thought landed like a hatchet to his chest. He'd hoped she'd get pregnant because he knew without a doubt that if she had, he wouldn't let her walk away. It had turned out his slow sperm hadn't done the trick after all, and he felt sorry for himself. "I get that it's time for you to move on, that I'll always just be another guy in a wheelchair that you've helped."

"Stop it right there!"

He'd obviously hit a sore spot.

"First of all, it's unlike you to feel sorry for yourself, so quit it. Second, how dare you make all these assumptions about me?" She'd given up staring at her feet and now impaled him with anger he'd seen often enough in the mirror. "How could we have *something* when you've never once told me you love me?"

Was that the problem? He didn't think they'd been in this bargain for love, so he'd kept his feelings at bay, and now she was blaming him? "I never heard those words from your mouth either," he fired back, feeling far too defensive, and immature, and knowing it was a pitiful comeback. Nevertheless, it was how he felt.

"You wouldn't have believed me if I'd said them," she said, so quietly he almost couldn't hear her. "You had things all wrapped up long before I arrived. You'd never trust anyone who dared fall for you in that chair. Why would I be so foolish to beat my head against that wall around your heart?"

In other words, he was the one who needed to have said it first. "I knew it was stupid to make that agreement. We played with fire, and now we've both been burned."

"You're the one who challenged me to prove it. Remember?"

What could he say? He'd challenged her—begged her, actually—and she'd given in to his demands. *Show me I'm still a man.* She'd asked for something in return, and he'd foolishly thought that would make their deal acceptable. All for sex. They'd owe each other nothing beyond the terms of their agreement. Wrong! Now he'd hurt her, and his mind was so messed up he didn't have a clue how to make things right. Yet one thought held firm. If she were pregnant, everything would be different. She watched him as he sat there without a single word to say beyond "I'm sorry, Mary."

"I can't stand the thought of these last two months being ruined by a silly argument."

"It's not so silly, is it?"

She sighed. "Like I said, it's not like we have another month to figure things out."

"True." He hated this moment, knowing she'd say goodbye and it could be another ten years before he saw her again. He reached for her hand and she let him take it. "Will you call me when you get there?"

"Sure."

He knew in his gut she wouldn't. They'd reached a truce. Nothing more. The word "love" wouldn't be uttered. For better or worse, they'd settled that.

She leaned over and kissed him. Unlike any of the other times, this was a parting kiss, and it tasted unbelievably bitter.

Then he sat there like one of those sculptures at the museum, and foolishly let her go.

CHAPTER TEN

One month later...

WES HAD FINISHED a thirty-minute procedure for carpal tunnel repair in outpatient surgery. He'd just successfully released the ligament over the affected nerve in the forty-year-old female patient's left wrist. If all went well, she'd soon be pain free, and the one-inch incision would heal and look like part of her "lifeline" on the palm.

Since returning to work, the head of his department, Ram Ramanathan, had suggested he cut his teeth with the shorter procedures. Thrilled to be back in the OR on any level, he'd agreed to start slowly and work his way back to the more complicated and time-consuming surgeries. The wrist nerve repairs were the perfect first step.

Even with the new "standing" wheelchair, he'd found being strapped into an upright position difficult to tolerate for long periods of time. Three to four carpal tunnel repairs were about all he could tolerate in a day. As most neurosurgeries took several hours, he was content to build up his tolerance, right there in day surgery. Most importantly, since returning to work he had distraction from his twenty-four-seven thoughts about Mary and how completely wrong he'd played his hand.

Returning the specially made wheelchair to the sitting position, he took a deep breath, and, glad to relieve the pressure around his chest, he rubbed the area, then released his legs from the thigh and shin straps. Though he couldn't feel his legs, he knew it was important to do some quick passive ROM exercises to help with circulation. After stripping off the dirty OR gown and gloves, he rolled into the post-surgical room and washed his hands.

A few minutes later, fresh scrubs donned under his white OR coat, he'd returned to his office for a few remaining appointments. As often happened, his mind drifted to the one who had got away, Mary. Instead of calling when she'd arrived in Astoria, like she'd promised, she'd merely mailed him a card. He still kept the envelope with her new address in his office desk drawer just to look at her writing, knowing her fingers had once touched it. Damn, he missed her.

In the card, Mary apologized for how things had turned out, then told him briefly about her new job. She'd stepped in as lead PT in a small hospital situated in a beautiful town tucked beside the Columbia River called Astoria. He could imagine her tiny house fitting in perfectly there, but hoped she didn't plan to stay there beyond the six weeks she'd agreed to in her work contract, while the regular lead PT took a cruise around the world.

Not wanting to mess up her plans, he'd kept his feelings to himself about how much he missed her, and wished beyond hope she'd come back. Instead, he'd sent a cordial yet contrite text message in response.

I'm sorry too. Glad you made it there safe and sound. Keep in touch.

What a jerk. He didn't deserve a great woman like Mary Harris. Not because he was in a wheelchair, but because at the age of thirty-seven he still didn't know how to love a woman the way she deserved. He wanted to. Was pretty damn sure Mary was the one person he could learn with, too.

He shook his head, remembering how he'd teased her about waiting for "that one special person". What had he known at the time? That had been before he'd finally gotten to know the most amazing woman in the world. Regardless, their relationship was out of his hands now. She worked in Oregon and he in California.

His computer lit up with an odd jingle. A video call. He considered ignoring the computer call—he'd explain later how busy he was—until he glanced at the monitor. Mary's name flashed.

Shaken, he quickly accepted the call, adrenaline suddenly perking him up. In a flutter of nerves he knocked the computer mouse off the desk. He quickly bent to pick it up, hoping he hadn't accidentally disconnected the call before it'd started. But when he sat back up, there was her beautiful face, on his computer monitor screen. She took his breath away, and he didn't have a second to prepare, yet there was so much he wanted to say.

No. She made the call. Let her talk first. See where it leads.

"Harris, how are you?" He did his best to sound casual but, with his pulse fluttering in his throat, he came off as anything but.

"I'm great. Beyond great." She definitely looked ecstatic, her eyes bright, shining with tears. Happy tears. "I wanted you to be the first to know, Wes."

"What? Is everything all right?"

She nodded vehemently. Some hair fell across her eyes, and she quickly brushed it away. "Couldn't be better. Perfect, in fact." She took a moment to compose herself. "So here's the news—you've held up your end of the bargain after all."

What? Now he really couldn't catch his breath. "You're…?"

"Yes," Again she nodded like a bobble head. "I'm pregnant!" She held a home pregnancy test strip, colored pink for positive, close to the computer camera for proof. "It's positive. I've tested two mornings in a row before calling just to make sure. We did it!" She pulled back the strip, her face coming into view again. Those bright green eyes broke into tears, though she grinned happily. "Thank you, Wes." She swiped at some of the tears making their way down her cheeks, but it was a futile gesture.

He wanted to touch her, to hold her in the worst way, to comfort her, hating the miles and the computer screen between them. Though frustrated with their separation at a time like this, tingles descended down his spine as he took in the significance of what she'd said. He'd fathered a child. He was going to be a father! A miracle, or meant to be?

Remembering their cold and calculated bargain, he kept cool. "One good swimmer, hey, Harris?"

She laughed, though he swore he could see a hint of sadness in her gaze. "Yes. All it took."

"Th-that's fantastic." What was he supposed to say? The woman he loved was pregnant with their baby. She'd bargained for that baby. Remember? She'd fallen in love with his niece Rose, and suddenly couldn't live without one of her own. He couldn't let her down by showing his true feelings. That he loved her and missed her and didn't know if he could go on without her. Or their baby.

Some strange yearning started building slowly, but he didn't have time to figure it out.

The new information certainly put an added spin on things, which had been complicated enough *before* her getting pregnant. Though shaken to the core, he pasted on his best happy face. Something he was sorely out of practice on. What the hell was he supposed to do now? *That's great. Carry on without me. Have a good life.* Damn it all to hell.

"I don't want to interfere with your work," she said, "but I've been bursting to tell you."

"You're not interfering." *Hang on to her as long as you can.* Though he did have an afternoon of appointments waiting. "I'm so glad you called."

"And I'm so happy you're back working. I was told you were in surgery this morning when I first called your office. That's wonderful. Everything we worked for we've accomplished."

"Even getting you pregnant." The biggest and most confusing shocker of all. That odd feeling seemed to be snowballing.

"Yes! Everything. Well, I won't keep you. I'll call again soon, though. I—"

Don't let her say it. Because then you'll have to be honest and tell her how you feel about her, and everything will change. Am I ready for that? Lover. Father. Husband?

"Uh, me, too, Harris. Me too."

Keep her wondering what I mean, and keep guessing what she was about to say.

"I love you" would have been his top choice. He'd had more than enough time to think about that unspoken phrase. Though long overdue, under the new circumstances, a baby, everything had changed!

She disconnected and her beautiful face disappeared from the screen. The room felt immediately empty, though the news had certainly knocked his socks off. She was pregnant!

He sat transfixed for several moments, considering his options. Theirs had been a bargain, both had gotten what they'd wanted. That should be that, right?

Not on your life. Everything had changed. He'd sworn the day she'd left that if she were pregnant everything would've been different. He wouldn't have let her leave. He wanted to be a father to his baby, not a long-distance parent but a dad every single day of his child's life. And because he'd fallen in love with her. When he finally told her, he needed to do it in person, not on some computer screen phone!

Wes picked up his work phone. "Ram? It's Wesley. Listen, I know I've only just come back to work. What's that? Yes, things are going very well, but I do have a problem. I need to take off a few days. I have some pressing business to take care of. No, it has nothing to do with my medical issues. I need to make a quick trip to Oregon. Could you ask Beverly to clear my schedule for the next few days?"

Once he'd hung up the phone, between seeing his afternoon patients he went online and booked the first flight to Portland, Oregon, for early the next morning. Then, when a patient failed to show for an appointment, he took advantage of the time to find a car rental that could accommodate his special need for hand controls. Because it was his first flight since becoming paraplegic, he decided to use the electric wheelchair to navigate the airport for greatest ease. But first, because he was back working and took his responsibility as a doctor seriously, he finished his remaining afternoon appointments in the clinic.

There were many obstacles complicating his getting to Mary the next day, but now that he'd come to his senses about what he needed and wanted to do, nothing would stop him. He grabbed the envelope in his desk with her new address, shoved it in his briefcase and rode out the office door.

Mary had had a particularly busy day and felt exhausted. The early pregnancy seemed to drain her of all her energy. And this was only the beginning. How would she handle it by herself when things got really tough?

Insecurity gripped her as she drove home.

Could she do everything alone? Wes had said he wanted to be involved, but how involved would that be? And he hadn't said a peep about any of that yesterday when she'd called. Maybe she'd made a mistake. Not on her life. She wanted this baby with every cell in her body. Knowing life was growing inside was the most thrilling sensation ever. She couldn't wait to hold her newborn in her arms. This bout of uncertainty had everything to do with hormones and nothing to do with her bold plans. She'd overcome a heck of a lot worse things in life. Having a baby would definitely take getting used to, but she'd find her support system and make it work. She had to.

She honestly didn't know what she'd expected when she'd called and told Wesley the news yesterday. A part of her, way inside her heart, had hoped he would propose on the spot. Stupid, wishful thoughts. She'd bargained for this baby and he'd certainly enjoyed his part of the process. Then she'd left abruptly. Hell, he could already be dating some new woman and moving on with his life. Either the thought or the hormones sickened her in a quick wave.

She pulled the pickup truck into the secluded driveway that led to a small man-made pond next to which she'd been lucky enough to park her tiny house. As she neared the cement pad where she hooked up to water and electricity, she saw an unfamiliar van. She parked on the opposite side of her house and when she got out she heard the other vehicle's doors slam shut.

Mary walked around to the front of her house and nearly stumbled and fell when she saw Wesley in his electric wheelchair, waiting for her. Her circulation took a dive from head to stomach at the sight. She needed to hold on to something, so she grabbed the porch railing to her house for support.

His coffee and cream eyes were guarded yet determined.

Still in shock, she managed to squeak out some words. "Wes! What are you doing here?"

"I love you. I need you. Figured it was about time I told you."

Positive she wouldn't be able to take a single step on such shaky legs, she clutched the wood tighter and stayed put.

He moved his electric wheelchair, covering half the distance between them. “You need me. Our baby needs us.” He managed a smile, his lips trembling nearly imperceptibly, but she could tell he was as nervous as she was. “Since you left I discovered there’s something much worse than being paraplegic. Loneliness. I don’t want a life without you.”

She swallowed against a paper-dry throat. Was she imagining this perfect moment?

“Let me be a real father to our child.” Her gaze shot upward, hardly able to believe what she was hearing. She tried to take a breath but could only manage a pant. He waited until her shock wore off and her eyes settled back on his. “Please.”

Wes had just said the fantasy words she’d been waiting and dying to hear all her life, but especially for the last two months. Oh, hell, she’d blame the sudden onset of tears on the hormones, as she knew too much information was about to flood out from her heart. She took a trial step toward him, still not trusting her legs. “I’ve loved you since I was fifteen, Wes.”

“Why didn’t you ever tell me?” He reached out

for her, his eyes softened and full of emotion but still stunned over what he'd just said, and she couldn't make herself move.

"I was afraid." Her hand flew to her stomach and her gaze dropped to the ground. "I never dared dream you could love a girl like me."

"A girl like you? You mean the most wonderful woman in my life?"

She looked at him again, unable to believe this moment was really happening. He'd shown up out of the blue from another state, which took some planning for a guy like him. He'd obviously been waiting for her. Now he'd confessed he loved her and wanted to be a part of her life.

How much more goodness could she take? Afraid she'd crumble if she let go, she held fast to the porch railing.

He studied her, an understanding expression on his face. Then he must have realized he hadn't said enough, even though he'd told her he loved her and wanted to be with her. Yes, she was that insecure where he was concerned.

So he began. "You were the first girl to ever take my breath away. At my sister's wedding, you looked more beautiful than the bride, and all I could think about was wanting to get you out of that dress. I was supposed to be engaged, but I couldn't think straight around you. What if, I thought, what if I went for it with Mary? Would she even want me?"

Her head spun with the information that would have changed the very course of her life back then. Why hadn't they gone for it?

"I've always been selfish, Harris, you know that. If I'd reached out for you then, if we'd gotten together, I would have blamed you for anything that went wrong." He dug fingers into now longer and fuller hair from the last time she'd seen him. She stood quiet, barely breathing, but taking in every word her spoke. Someday she'd want to savor these moments again, so she needed to memorize his face and what he was saying.

"Hell, I might have been like my father and blamed you for my becoming a paraplegic. Who knows? Because I didn't know how to open my heart up and love someone back then." He moved closer, dividing their distance by half again, until she could see the self-doubt in his eyes and the longing to make her understand. She began to relax, her fingers letting go of their death-like clutch on the wood railing.

"The point is, Harris, I've changed, and you're the one who changed me. You showed up uninvited and wouldn't take no for an answer, and I couldn't for the life of me understand why you stuck around. I was horrible to you, because you mixed me up, made me remember old feelings. Hell, I was in a wheelchair, what good were old feelings anyway? But you wouldn't let me get away with excuses. I started waking up every morning looking forward to seeing you, to getting to know you all over again.

"I was shocked how much you'd changed. How confident and skilled you were. How beautiful and sexy. My God, I couldn't quit thinking about you, and it bugged the hell out of me. What was the point? Why fall for the most lovable lady on the planet when nothing could come of it?

"You led me back to the living, and we made our pact with the devil, and, heaven help me, you made me feel like a man again. You may have thought I wasn't man enough to tell you how I really felt but the truth was I didn't want to trap you or tie you down with me. What did I have to offer you?"

She whimpered, sadness draining her, remembering their tragic and complicated story, the one she'd thought through a thousand times but had never come up with a satisfying ending to, until today. Until right now.

"The point of all this is everything has changed. I finally realize I love you with all my heart and soul, but only because you taught me how to love in the first place." A tiny ironic laugh slipped through his lips. "You once called me your life-changer. Well, it's you who changed me, and I love you for it, and I want with everything I have to be a real father to our baby, not just some sperm donor."

She drew her fist to her mouth, trying not to sob. He was for real. There was no doubting his intentions or sincerity.

"But the big question is, since you're still hugging those railings and I'm laying my guts on the line for you, will you have me? For better or worse?" He gestured toward his legs and the wheelchair. "The future won't be easy with me, but I want to go there with you. If you'll let me."

She broke free from her hold and rushed to him, then melted into his arms and folded herself onto his lap. "I love you more than you can ever understand, because I've never stopped loving you since the first day I met you. There's no changing a young girl's heart." She kissed him, getting his cheeks as wet as hers. "I love your stubbornness and your pride and even your arrogance. I love your resilience and intelligence, but most of all I love you being a big enough man to admit you didn't know how to love."

She threw her arms around his neck and squeezed tight. "I'm so happy to be the one to teach you, because you helped me, too, to love like I never believed I could. We ventured into that wilderness together with our crazy bargain, and, man, what a shocker. I love you, not because you're the best lover I've ever had but because you're the best man I've ever met. Sitting or standing. You're the one, and I don't ever plan to stop loving you, because I never have yet, and you've given me plenty of good reasons."

They laughed together, him being self-deprecating, further proof he was a changed man. Then they kissed again, this one not full of fire but more like a solemn vow, a sweet promise of all the great things to come.

Wes's fingers stroked her cheek. "You said I could still have it all, and I want it all, but only with you…and our baby." He tenderly planted his hand on her stomach. "Let's prove it, Harris. Marry me."

How could she not take him up on his dare? "I'd love to."

His confident smile soon turned cocky. "Aren't you going to invite me in?"

She lifted a brow, then slipped off his lap and took him home.

EPILOGUE

Eighteen months later...

"WHOA, WHOA, WHOA!"

Henry Van Allen was the spitting image of his father, with dark hair and shining eyes, and at ten months he was determined to prove he could walk. He tottered, breaking away from the coffee table in the waiting room, and took four drunken steps toward Wes in his wheelchair. Then stopped.

Mary clapped her hands, egging him on. "Come on, come to Momma." She bent forward and held out her hands while walking backward. Henry stood still, as though considering his options, then went for it and made a dozen more steps in quick order across the doctor's waiting-room carpet before landing on his diaper-padded bottom. He pouted and cried, and Mary rushed to pick him up.

"Do you know how proud I am of you? You can walk! Such a big boy." She hugged him then put him on his father's lap.

"Trying to show up your old man already, huh?" He proudly squeezed the boy, who always ate up any and all attention from his dad.

A physical therapist appeared at the door and invited them all in to the therapy room. "Are you ready, Dr. Van Allen?"

"As ready as I'm ever going to be."

"Have a seat right there."

A regular chair awaited him, but on the chair was something that looked like a jet pack, and extending down, connected to the back apparatus, were serious-looking leg braces. They called it an exoskeleton and it had cost as much as a new sports car, but with Wes, money was not the object, walking was.

Once he transferred from his wheelchair to the other chair, the PT assistant helped him slip the straps over his shoulders. He snapped them tight at his sternum. She moved down to his thighs and then around his knees to two other sets of braces and fasteners. Once secured, she handed him two long rubber-tipped canes with braces for his elbows and hands, the hand sections with sensors.

The PT held a small box of controls in her hands. "Once you get the hang of walking again, you'll be able to control your steps all by yourself."

"I'm ready."

Mary had never seen her husband look more determined in her life. She snuggled a squirmy Henry and held her breath as Wes prepared to take one small step for himself, but a huge step for his future.

The PT stayed close behind him and fiddled with the control panel and, to her amazement, Mary saw her husband stand. Soon he was taking natural-looking steps, with his knees bending and heels touching the floor in a perfectly normal gait.

Henry squirmed to get down so he could go to his father. Mary held his pudgy hands to keep him from falling.

"Once you're more familiar with the technology, you'll be able to control your walking using the sensors in the canes."

Wes glanced up at Mary with an amazed expression. "Can you believe it? I'm walking!"

"Daddy's walking!" She watched excitedly as Henry tagged alongside him. "You and Henry have a lot in common."

He laughed good-naturedly, as that sweetest part of his personality had grown exponentially since they'd married and he'd become a father. "I think Henry might already be doing a better job of walking than me, though." He truly had become a new man, starting first from the inside out, and now, with his standing and walking the length of the PT room right before her eyes with the help of the robotic skeleton, proved it.

"You're doing great, Dr. Van Allen. How about once more around the room then we'll let you try it out all by yourself."

Wesley looked at his wife, walking beside him with their wavy-haired, chubby and sturdy boy, and had never felt prouder in his life. He and Mary were eye to eye for a change—without being vertical on a bed. Actually, he was a good foot taller than her now that he was standing. He'd spent the last couple of years looking up at people's chins and nostrils and, to be honest, he'd gotten sick of the view. But not tired of looking at Mary, he'd never get tired of looking at Mary. Or Henry.

A couple of months ago he'd found an online video of a lady taking her first steps after being paraplegic for over twenty years. With Mary's eager blessing, he'd soon been measured for his very own exoskeleton. Now here he was, showing off for his kid, who had taken a break and sat down, now playing pat-a-cake and gurgling as he watched his dad take his first steps around the room.

Once Mary had told him she was pregnant, and she'd wrapped up her contract in Astoria, he'd convinced her to come back to Malibu and marry him immediately.

Within the month they'd had a small wedding in his living room for family and a few friends, with the Pacific Ocean as a backdrop at sunset. He'd never forget for as long as he lived how beautiful she'd looked in a simple white Grecian-styled satin gown, her shining hair flowing free over her shoulders, with a delicate wreath of baby's breath flowers around her head and holding white roses. He'd hardly been able to believe she would be his from that day forward.

Wearing a white tux and sitting in his special standing wheelchair, he'd flipped a switch and, thanks to a smooth hydraulic system, he'd literally risen to the occasion to take their wedding vows upright. Eye to eye.

He wouldn't have believed their lovemaking could have gotten any better after saying *I do*, but that night, making love as man and wife, he'd been overcome with emotion, fully understanding the precious gift he'd been given in the form of Mary Harris. Wondering why it had taken him twenty years to figure it out, but finally understanding how transformative love could be. All he could say was that he was one lucky guy.

And their life together had only looked up. Within a few short months he'd happily picked up his full career as a neurosurgeon, and he was back to his prior booming practice. Surgery and all. Meanwhile, Mary had quickly found a part-time job nearby, which had also given her plenty of time to plan, paint and decorate the nursery. And soon, as the good book his grandmother used to read to him at Christmas said, she was great with child.

In fact, she'd looked fantastic pregnant. In her case, she'd truly glowed and beamed with life. He'd taken all the birthing classes with her and had been at her side through a long and grueling labor. When she'd become exhausted and about to give up, their boy had finally popped out his head, already crying before the rest of his body had even been born. And if marriage wasn't adventure enough, parenting had been the toughest yet most rewarding thing he could ever imagine. The kid was theirs! Plus he loved the fact his genes were clearly dominant in the boy.

His son, so far, only knew him as being in a wheelchair, yet today he'd stood and walked. He might look like an astronaut on the moon with the computer-directed steps, but it was a start. He believed in scientific innovation and had read a few successful studies using functional electrical stimulation to restore muscle movements. These were all temporary fixes, but he believed in the power of neuroscience and robotics and figured it was only a matter of time before they'd be able to implant a tiny computer with sensor-stimulators along the injured sections of the spine.

Until then, his job was to keep himself in good shape. With a wife like Mary, he had no doubt he'd be in top-notch condition for the rest of his life.

For now, though, he'd settle for this clunky walking suit.

"Are you ready to try it on your own?"

He looked at Mary and winked. "Hell, yeah, let's get on with it. I want to dance with my wife on our second anniversary."

Wes grinned, full of bravado, then, showing off for his wife and kid, he used the hand sensors on the canes and took himself for a slow but steady stroll for the first time in nearly three years.

And the best part of all was hearing his baby boy say, "Yay. Dada. Yay."

* * * * *

If you enjoyed this story, check out these other great reads from Lynne Marshall

WEDDING DATE WITH THE ARMY DOC
HIS PREGNANT SLEEPING BEAUTY
A MOTHER FOR HIS ADOPTED SON
FATHER FOR HER NEWBORN BABY
HOT-SHOT DOC, SECRET DAD

All available now!

MILLS & BOON®
Large Print Medical

December

Healing the Sheikh's Heart	Annie O'Neil
A Life-Saving Reunion	Alison Roberts
The Surgeon's Cinderella	Susan Carlisle
Saved by Doctor Dreamy	Dianne Drake
Pregnant with the Boss's Baby	Sue MacKay
Reunited with His Runaway Doc	Lucy Clark

January

The Surrogate's Unexpected Miracle	Alison Roberts
Convenient Marriage, Surprise Twins	Amy Ruttan
The Doctor's Secret Son	Janice Lynn
Reforming the Playboy	Karin Baine
Their Double Baby Gift	Louisa Heaton
Saving Baby Amy	Annie Claydon

February

Tempted by the Bridesmaid	Annie O'Neil
Claiming His Pregnant Princess	Annie O'Neil
A Miracle for the Baby Doctor	Meredith Webber
Stolen Kisses with Her Boss	Susan Carlisle
Encounter with a Commanding Officer	Charlotte Hawkes
Rebel Doc on Her Doorstep	Lucy Ryder

MILLS & BOON®
Large Print Medical

March

The Doctor's Forbidden Temptation	Tina Beckett
From Passion to Pregnancy	Tina Beckett
The Midwife's Longed-For Baby	Caroline Anderson
One Night That Changed Her Life	Emily Forbes
The Prince's Cinderella Bride	Amalie Berlin
Bride for the Single Dad	Jennifer Taylor

April

Sleigh Ride with the Single Dad	Alison Roberts
A Firefighter in Her Stocking	Janice Lynn
A Christmas Miracle	Amy Andrews
Reunited with Her Surgeon Prince	Marion Lennox
Falling for Her Fake Fiancé	Sue MacKay
The Family She's Longed For	Lucy Clark

May

The Spanish Duke's Holiday Proposal	Robin Gianna
The Rescue Doc's Christmas Miracle	Amalie Berlin
Christmas with Her Daredevil Doc	Kate Hardy
Their Pregnancy Gift	Kate Hardy
A Family Made at Christmas	Scarlet Wilson
Their Mistletoe Baby	Karin Baine

1117 LP 2P P2 Medical